Learning to Dance

and Other Stories
by Sharon Oard Warner

Sharon Oard Warner

Santa Fe, NM   Sept. 19, 200_

For P.J. —
(sorry!)

With my best
wishes. I enjoyed
meeting you. Write your
book!

Sharon

Minnesota Voices Project Number 52

NEW RIVERS PRESS 1992

Copyright © 1992 by Sharon Oard Warner
Library of Congress Catalog Card Number 91-61257
ISBN 0-89823-132-9
All Rights Reserved
Edited by Susan Welch
Editorial Assistance by Paul J. Hintz
Cover artwork and design by Barbara Robinette Moss
Book Design by Gaylord Schanilec
Typesetting by Peregrine Publications

The publication of *Learning to Dance and Other Stories* has been made possible by grants from the Jerome Foundation and the Metropolitan Regional Arts Council (from an appropriation by the Minnesota Legislature). Additional support has been provided by the Arts Development Fund of the United Arts Council, the First Bank System Foundation, Liberty State Bank, the Star Tribune/Cowles Media Company, the Tennant Company Foundation, and the National Endowment for the Arts (with funds appropriated by the Congress of the United States). New Rivers Press also wishes to acknowledge the Minnesota Non-Profits Assistance Fund for its invaluable support.

New Rivers Press books are distributed by

The Talman Company
150 Fifth Avenue
New York, NY 10011

Bookslinger
2402 University Avenue West
Saint Paul, MN 55114

Learning to Dance and Other Stories has been manufactured in the United States of America for New Rivers Press, 420 N. 5th Street/Suite 910, Minneapolis, MN 55401 in a first edition of 2,000 copies.

Contents

Acknowledgements

Front Cover: Denver Art Museum Collection. "The Dance Examination (Examen de Danse)" by Edgar Degas.

"Fools Fall in Love" © Butch Hancock. Rainlight Music (ASCAP). Used with permission.

"London Homesick Blues" written by Gary P. Nunn, © Nunn Publishing Company. Used with permission.

Some of the stories in *Learning to Dance* have previously appeared in somewhat different versions in the following publications: *The Gamut, Green Mountains Review, Iowa Woman, The Long Story,* and *Sonora Review.* Our thanks to the editors of these publications for allowing us to reprint the stories here.

The author wishes to express her thanks to Susan Welch, for her careful editing and advice; to Barbara Robinette Moss, for her artistic vision and generous support; and to C. W. Truesdale and Katie Maehr, for all the work they've done on behalf of this book.

For Teddy

BLANCHE: Whoever you are—
I have always depended on the
kindness of strangers.

—from A Streetcar Named Desire
by Tennessee Williams

The Whole World at Once

Laura is on her way home from school when she hears the rumble of a car coming slowly up the street behind her. Because she is an only child and small for fourteen, her father is protective; each morning as she goes out the door he warns her not to take chances. Drowsy and ready to be on her way, Laura doesn't bother to listen, but she carries his voice away with her. She hears it now, competing with the sound of the approaching car for her attention. When the car finally slides into view it's only an old white Chevrolet with a quivering hood and a young woman driver who looks Laura straight in the eye. Relieved, Laura stops to redistribute the weight of the backpack she has slung over one shoulder. She moves the clarinet case from her right hand to her left and walks on.

The clarinet is on loan from the band director. Laura's instrument is the flute, but girls all over school play the flute as well or better than she does. The band director was straight with her this afternoon. He said if she wants a chance at marching band, which she does, she'll have to play the clarinet. Just a simple adjustment, he told her, no more difficult than making a new friend. He suggested that she take the clarinet home and "see if it speaks to you." She is almost sure it won't, but part of her hopes she will lift the instrument from the case to her lips and play brilliantly on the spot. Mr. Andrews, the band director, has blonde hair and the most amazing blue eyes. She imagines them fixed on her while she plays for him, all surprise and admiration. She knows he's wrong about making friends, though. Her best friend, Jenny, moved suddenly last August, and in the two months since school started, Laura has walked the halls pretty much alone.

The Chevrolet is idling down at the corner stop sign by the Methodist Church. The license plate hangs askew and flaps weakly against the fender when the car starts to move again. Laura thinks the Chevrolet may be as old as she is. Blue-black exhaust billows out as it turns the corner and disappears. The smoke hangs in the air, reminding Laura of magic tricks and Walt Disney movies. As a little girl, she loved Sleeping Beauty and Snow White. The Halloween she was nine, Laura dressed as Snow White. She remembers the costume her mother made with the white standup collar and blue capped sleeves. Before Laura went out trick or treating, her mother smoothed her hair into a Snow White pageboy and sprayed it stiff with lacquer. Her father took a picture of her standing on the porch, clasping a red apple in her hand. It's in the album. Laura came across it recently, but the snapshot might have been of any little girl. Her father always stands so far back with his camera that all his photographs end up looking pretty much the same, tiny figures frozen smack in the middle of a much bigger picture. Tightening her grasp on the clarinet case, Laura watches the exhaust rise into the gray sky. Halloween is next week. Some houses already have carved pumpkins on their steps.

The sputtering resumes behind her, and she knows without turning that the Chevrolet is back again. She's about a block from home when the car makes a wide U turn in the middle of the street and pulls over beside her, coming so close that the whitewalls scrape the curb. Laura takes a few more steps then stops and looks over at the car. The girl in the driver's seat is struggling with a gearshift on the steering wheel, and while Laura watches, she does something that fills the street with an ugly, grinding noise. Framed by the open window, her face looks young and a little lost, as though she's only recently gotten her driver's license and has strayed too far from home. Laura relaxes and gets ready to give directions. She has lived in this neighborhood most of her life and knows her way around.

"Hi," the driver says, smiling a little. Her red hair is a mass of long, coiled curls springing up around her head in every direction.

When the breeze catches them, the curls seem to come alive, dancing about the girl's still face.

"Hi," Laura echoes in a small voice. She has never seen such a head of hair, and she can't decide whether it looks wonderful or terrible.

"Do you babysit?" the driver asks.

Laura nods. Babysitting is a recent enthusiasm. She's been sitting since early summer for the next door neighbor, a woman who already has two small children and is pregnant with a third. Laura was surprised the first time she visited her neighbor's house. She had always assumed everyone else lived the same sort of orderly existence she does, clean floors and dinner at six. Not so. Just last week Laura had to fish a toy boat out of the toilet before she could sit down. Her neighbor's closet doors are always wide open, and the children run in and out of all the rooms. At first, the disorder confused her, but now she hardly notices it. What Laura remembers most about her visits next door is the pleasant tickling in her throat when the three-year-old girl sits in her lap and combs through her hair.

"What about babies?" the driver asks in a strange voice, as though she is trying to discover something. For the first time, Laura looks into the driver's eyes. Large and brown, they're rimmed with red in a permanent sort of way, as though she's been either ill or sad for a long time.

"I love babies," Laura replies, realizing that it's true, that it must be true of all girls her age, girls who have given up dolls but have yet to take up boys.

The driver doesn't look convinced. "Have you ever taken care of a baby?" she asks.

"Not yet," Laura admits, "but I have a neighbor who is pregnant, and I'm going to take care of her baby when it's born. She's giving me lessons." This last part is not true.

"Well, then," the driver goes on, sounding like some lawyer on television, "what do you do after you give a baby a bottle?" Her face is scrunched up, as though she were looking into the sun. Actually, the sky is overcast and wintry looking.

"You hold it up against your shoulder," Laura answers, raising the clarinet case to demonstrate. "And you pat its back until it burps."

3

She pats the case and thinks of the clarinet, safe and snug inside.

"And if the baby cries?" the driver goes on, ignoring the case pressed against Laura's chest, rushing ahead as though this were a test with a time limit.

"What do you mean?" Laura asks.

"What if the baby cries?" the driver says stubbornly. She glances at Laura and then looks away at something that has caught her interest in the car. Carefully, Laura lowers the case to the sidewalk, then straightens and folds her arms across her chest.

"You pick it up," she says. "You check the diaper, try a bottle, rock for a little while. Babies can't say what they want. You have to experiment."

The driver's face relaxes. "You're right," she says to Laura, nodding her head until the curls shift about her face. Her skin is pale, and Laura is reminded of those ancient statues, the ones that don't have arms but whose faces are still perfectly beautiful, even after hundreds and hundreds of years.

"Do you need a babysitter for this weekend?" Laura asks, making a list in her head of the things she has to do. There's the clarinet, of course, plus a history test to study for. And on Saturdays her mother insists on chores. She wants Laura to learn responsibility, which means redoing things her mother has already done, vacuuming a carpet that still shows signs of having been vacuumed the day before, mopping an already spotless floor. "Do you know how late you'll be? My mother is . . . "

"Would you like to see her?" the driver asks, looking down in her lap again. Suddenly, Laura realizes the girl is holding a baby, that she was driving with a baby in her lap. No wonder she was creeping down the street, Laura thinks.

Nodding, she shrugs the backpack further over her shoulder and walks quickly to the car window. Sure enough, the baby is nestled in the folds of the driver's skirt. As Laura watches, the baby's eyes open and then close again, the irises an inky blue, the gaze unfocused and wavering. Laura can't remember ever seeing a baby this new, one with tightly curled fists and legs drawn up so that the tiny feet wave in the air like flowers. Except for the pink, quilted overalls and socks, except for the blue bruise in the center of her forehead, this baby might still be floating in her own quiet bubble. Laura leans closer and releases her breath. "She's so beautiful," she hears herself say. Laura's mother has a saying that all babies are sweet, but they aren't all beautiful. She tells the story of how shocked she was when Laura was born, how no one had warned her that newborns don't look like the babies in magazines, that their heads are misshapen and their skin is red and wrinkled. This baby's skin is milky, and on her round head she has the fuzzy beginnings of red hair. "How old is she?" Laura asks.

"Six days," says the mother. "She was born about this time six days ago."

"It's not my business," Laura says, "but shouldn't she be in a car seat?"

"Babies are everyone's business," the mother replies; then she grasps the baby under the arms and hoists her into the air. Even so, the baby's legs stay firmly drawn. "I knew you were responsible." she says, turning her gaze to Laura. "I could tell by the way you carry your instrument. You wouldn't drop her, not for the world."

Laura starts to say that the clarinet is not hers, but she doesn't have time. The mother quickly kisses her baby, firm on the mouth, then holds her out the window.

"Take her," she says. Laura hesitates, but she hates the way the baby is dangling so far from the ground, nothing under her but the cement curb. Reaching out, she feels the quilted overalls, then the tiny rib cage, shrinking and expanding beneath her fingers. For an instant, she has hold of one of the mother's hands, too. It's warm, warmer even than the baby, and quivering. With a little groan, the mother pulls free, shrinking back into her car. "Hold her close," she tells Laura.

Obedient, Laura tries doing with the baby what she did with the clarinet case and is surprised to feel the baby nestling against her, head on her shoulder, breath warming her neck. She realizes that she's been chilly standing there, that winter is coming on fast. "Her name is Nicole," says the driver, and Laura is repeating the name in a squeaky voice when she hears the grinding of gears and the boom of the old engine taking off. The white Chevrolet pulls away with a squeal, fast, as though the driver were getting onto the expressway.

"Hey, wait," Laura cries, but it's no good. The car has disappeared, leaving Laura and the baby in a cloud of smoke. The smell of burning oil fills the street, and Laura thinks it can't be healthy for a baby to breathe such fumes. Relaxing her grip a little, she nudges the baby's face into her collar before moving back to the sidewalk and the black clarinet case. She studies the case for a few seconds then lets the backpack slide down her arm until it drops to the pavement beside the case. Her things look odd lying there, as though Laura has run away or been abducted and, in her rush, has left everything behind. She knows what her father would say: She's taking chances with her belongings; anyone could come along and steal them. She hesitates, then begins down the sidewalk with the baby. It's all right, she tells herself, her father can't expect her to carry home the whole world at once.

Working Puzzles

Some lessons have to be learned over and over. What we don't like we tend to forget.

I do remember being six years old and lying in darkness, my eyes on hundreds of milling lights. Bits of neon, they flew in multi-colored swarms about my room, and for lack of another name, I called them "bugs." Sometimes I would lie quietly and watch them until I went off to sleep. Usually, though, I called my father. The bugs weren't threatening, but I was troubled that no one else could see them. The ritual was for Daddy to shoo them into a corner behind the door, corralling a few, so that I could point at first one, then another. "Here's a red one," I'd say. "Do you see it?" I was sure that if my pointing were exact enough, he'd relent and say yes. He never did, though. Eventually, he'd shrug his shoulders and sigh, as though he'd done his best. Then, he'd pick me up and carry me back to bed. "Close your eyes," he'd whisper. "That way you won't see them." What was the point of telling him that they swirled in the darkness behind my eyelids? Even then, I knew there were places he couldn't go.

In March of 1959, while I was in first grade and concentrating on other things, my parents separated. Divorce was not so common then. I had never heard of it before it happened to me. Little girls from other classes cornered me in the bathroom and asked frightening questions: how would we eat? where would we live? I had visions

7

of a tornado touching down on the roof of our house, scattering us and our possessions to the four winds.

Actually, the dispersal was a good deal more orderly. Mother, my four-year-old brother Sonny, and I moved to the other side of Dallas, a big jump even then. Mother must have answered an ad in the paper because we took up living with two strangers, a woman, Meda, and her grown daughter. Their house was in the country, just off the intersection of two farm roads that seemed to go there and then on to nowhere. A mimosa tree sprawled across the front yard, and I loved to lie under it and stare up through the twisted branches. When we moved to Meda's, the tree was heavy with long curling pods. Our first days there, I distracted myself by gathering the pods in the skirt of my dress. I would sit on the porch and split them open, dividing the flat green peas – some for Meda's daughter, Linda; some for Sonny; some for the dogs. I chewed a few gritty seeds myself and was tormented afterwards by the thought of seedlings attaching themselves to my stomach and winding their blind way up my throat.

Sonny and I stayed outdoors as much as possible. Meda's house was dark and silent. No matter what the day was like outside, inside it was always the same: The blinds were closed, and lightbulbs burned. In the den and dining room, dark paneling absorbed the available light. The house had that sour, closed-up smell children hate.

Meda boarded and bred dogs for a living. She boarded any sort of dog, but she bred Pekingese. Cages were stashed around the house and along the walls of the garage: chicken wire cages; wooden cages; cages with doors and tiny latches; and gathering dust in the corner of the dining room, a wrought-iron bird cage, birdless. A kennel stretched down the middle of the backyard, a long concrete rectangle that housed up to twenty dogs. Each dog had a tiny indoor area just big enough to lie down in and a small fenced patio outdoors for pacing. Like most little girls, I was drawn to small spaces and wanted to convert one of the pens into a playhouse. When I got up the nerve to ask, my mother snorted and Meda laughed out loud; the answer, I understood, was no.

Like my brother and me, the dogs preferred the outdoors. Some stood for hours on their little patios, snouts pressed to the chain-link fence, eyes roaming the fields to the strip of road, hunting that familiar car. Loyal, they never thought to hold a grudge. When their owners returned, they became happy circus dogs: barking, twirling, leaping into the air. As soon as they'd run through their tricks, though, they expected to be released, and if Meda weren't quick about it, they became desperate and hurled themselves against the fence. Once out of the cage, they resumed their circus antics and ran in dizzy circles around the pair of legs that had come to retrieve them. I often wondered whether they remembered that these were the same legs that had brought them to Meda's in the first place.

Other dogs did remember. Until we moved to Meda's, I never knew a dog could go hoarse from barking the way people do from screaming. I remember one in particular that barked, then yelped, and after a day or so, was reduced to a noisy wheeze. When I went out to visit him, he was curled in one corner, his bowls of water and food untouched. I kneeled beside his cage, poked my hand through a hole in the chain link and spoke soft, soothing words, but he only eyed me wearily and sighed a deep dog sigh. He was a curly-haired black spaniel, and to this day, the sweet sadness of childhood washes over me every time I see one. When the owners of these miserable dogs returned, Meda would pull them aside and explain how the dog had grieved and how she had done her best to console him. (Actually, she treated them all the same — feeding, watering, cleaning the cages, and giving each a brief pat on the head.) The guilty owners went from Meda to the cage. Crouching, they would call to their pets, but the dogs often refused to move. They'd become comfortable in their misery and didn't want a change of scene, certainly not if it meant delivering themselves back into the hands of the traitor. Eventually, though, Meda and the owners prevailed, even if it meant that Meda had to crawl into the cage and nudge the dog to its freedom.

Some dogs managed to be happy whatever their predicament. Happy to arrive, happy to leave, happy in between. These dogs ate their food noisily, barked at squirrels and at each other, and licked my fingers through the fence. I visited these happy ones both morning and evening and was sorry to see them go. I especially liked to sit in the damp grass beside their patios, arms around my knees, breathing in the noisy pleasure of them.

I shared a room with Linda. She was twenty-one, nearly twenty-

9

two, when we met, but she seemed my age, would have seemed my age regardless of how old I'd been. She was empathic and thus ageless. Because of severe cerebral palsy, Linda could do very little for herself. Meda lifted her from bed in the morning and returned her to bed at night. She carried Linda to and from the bathroom, brought her food on trays and retrieved the empty dishes. In the morning, Meda squatted beside the wheelchair and pulled booties onto Linda's twisted feet. The booties were knit from heavy wool, blue or red, with large pompoms that shifted about whenever Linda moved. I was fascinated by those booties. They were like baby shoes for an enormous doll. On the one hand, it hurt me that Linda had to wear them, and I considered stuffing them in the trash for her. On the other hand, I wished I could wear a pair myself.

We slept in twin beds, separated by the desk where Linda did her jigsaw puzzles. Her wheelchair was usually parked between us, and when I got up in the middle of the night to go to the bathroom, I had to remember to feel for it in the dark. One night I was still wide awake long after every else in the house was asleep, so I got out of bed and crept into Linda's big chair. The seat sagged, and when I sat down it folded up around me like a sling. My feet dangled above the metal foot rests. I wondered whether Linda had owned smaller chairs and what had become of them when she outgrew them. Had Meda presented the chairs as gifts, the way parents often do with necessities like clothes? I saw myself wheeling about in a smaller version, a red bow strapped across the back, the tails of the ribbon trailing across the hardwood floor as I rolled slowly from room to room. Pressing my fingers against the smooth rubber wheels, I inched forward, and with effort made my way to the end of the bed. If I were Linda, I knew that I would seldom go farther. There were days when she never left the room except to go across the hall to the bathroom, and that in her mother's arms.

Just as I was about to climb down, I noticed one shining bug slowly circling the room. In a minute more, hundreds swirled in lazy arcs around me. I kept my eyes on them, straining forward with my feet for the ground. "Oh no," I whispered, my heart pounding wildly, my fingers clutching the smooth rubber wheels. More than anything, I wanted to call for my daddy, but I knew that if I did, it would be

Mother who'd come, and she'd be angry that I had pulled her from sleep with his name.

When I began to cry Linda's voice rose out of the darkness. "It's okay," she said. Speaking wasn't easy for her; nothing was. She had to concentrate, and even so, her words came out sounding as though they'd been punched and stretched into a slightly different shape. For the first few weeks, I'd had to mull over everything she said, sending the sounds back through my head as an echo until I could make sense of them. Then one day her words were suddenly clear, and I was happy to stand by and wait while she went through the effort it took to form them.

"I want my daddy," I told her that night. I was wriggling slowly to the floor, but the vinyl seat clung to my skin and hindered my progress.

"Of course you do," she replied.

Though the bugs still swirled around the dark edges of the room, Linda's voice pushed them out to a breathable distance. I focused on one, twisting in the seat to chart its progress. Were these the same bugs that had visited me in my daddy's house, I wondered, and if they were, how had they followed me here? In my mind I saw my mother's old paneled station wagon careening down the highway, bright bugs streaming out behind in long ribbons. "I'm afraid of the dark, Linda," I said.

"Of course you are," her voice came back.

* * *

Each day a big yellow school bus picked me up across the street from Meda's house. When I saw it coming, I'd step back into the ditch. The driver resented slowing down and kept us children humble by making last-minute stops. We might have been hitchhikers and him the reluctant Good Samaritan. "Come on, come on," he'd mutter as we struggled up the steps with lunchboxes and books. Except for conceding to pick us up, he ignored us completely. We could have done any crazy thing we wanted — hanging out windows, throwing books — except that we had to sit tight and hold on to keep from being thrown into the aisle. At first, this wild ride was frightening, but after a while I enjoyed barreling across the countryside. I got familiar with the ruts, and the driver was predictable in his madness. Every day, morning and afternoon, he'd look away from the road to a certain white house nearly hidden by heavy willows. The house was situated on a curve, and as he came up on it, he'd swerve first toward and then away, throwing the bus and all us children off balance. I got to where I looked for that house. I thought he'd stop one day, and go inside to settle whatever it was that made him crazy, leaving all of us to climb out and play beneath the trees.

One afternoon when I got off the bus, Sonny was waiting by the side of the road. He was only four and spent his days with Meda and Linda while Mother shuttled between three or four part time jobs, different ones all the time, so that I gave up asking where she was going. Before the divorce, Sonny and I had slept together in a double bed, but now that we'd moved to Meda's, he shared a room with Mother and spent his time in the garage. Mother asked me to check on him from time to time, but he was always doing the same thing: wandering about the dark edges of the room, transferring his toys from one empty cage to another. Occasionally, when we'd cross paths in the dark hall, he'd lunge for me and sink his small teeth into my upper arm. Because he bit me, I knew we were still related, and unless he drew blood, I only slapped him a little and went on.

"Linda," he breathed, his chest heaving as though he'd been running. I looked at him closely and ran for the house.

Linda was in bed. At first, I thought she must be sick, but as soon as she saw me she turned her face to the wall. Edging into the room, I smelled the urine that had soaked the sheets and noticed she was still wearing the same pink nightgown Meda had put on her the night before. "Linda?" I said, moving close enough to touch the dull gold of her hair.

She wouldn't look at me. "Mother's been drinking," she said. "Please try to get her up."

Sonny waited in the hall. He was crying, and the neck of his T-shirt was stretched and wrinkled. I took his hand, and he led me down the hall to Meda's room.

Meda was in bed, too, stretched diagonally across the mattress. Her top sheet, bedspread, and pillows had been tossed about the room;

on one of the pillows a Pekingese perched like a queen's pet. Outside, the day was dazzling, and sunlight leaked between the slats of the blinds, filtered in, as through water. Wearing only her underwear, her arms and legs thrown out against the faded blue sheet, Meda looked as though she were swimming through some small, protected cove. Swimming, or maybe drowning.

"Meda?" I said in a quiet voice. When she didn't move, I crouched beside the bed, close enough so I could feel her breath and see the tiny hairs moving inside her nose. Her head was turned to one side, and the slit of a scab on the back of her neck was visible.

Meda kept her hair short, chopped off around her ears like a man's. She cut it herself with sewing scissors. I'd sat on the edge of the tub and watched her do it just the week before. To clip the back, she'd used a hand mirror. Her strong hand had cut a straight line across the back of her neck, and even after she'd slipped and sliced into her skin, raising a thin line of blood, she had gone on wielding the scissors with the same assurance. Fascinated, I had held my breath, thinking she might hack off one ear and go right on cutting. When she was finished, she turned and smiled at me, one of those thin pretend smiles adults wear for children.

"What do you think?" she'd asked. She was looking right at me, but I could still see the back of her head in the mirror and the slash of the cut. A drop of blood made its slow way toward her collar. I didn't know which to pay attention to, the front of her head or the back. "Well?" she prompted.

Her hair was short — no nonsense, no style — not much different from my own. I wanted long hair, preferably in braids, but my mother insisted on the boyish cut she called a "pixie."

"When I grow up I'm going to have long hair," I said.

"You have no idea what you'll do when you grow up," Meda had replied.

Passed out on the bed, she looked much older than when she was tending the dogs.

"Meda," I said, then louder, "Meda," until I was all but screaming in her ear. She moaned and thrashed around a bit and looked as though she really were drowning. I felt sorry for her and wanted to cover her with a sheet and go away, but whenever I fell silent, the sound of Linda's crying filtered down the hall.

"Sonny," I called, "go get me a pan of water." Usually, he argued when I bossed him around, but this time he turned and ran from the room. While I waited for him, I sank down at the foot of the bed, pulled Meda's sheets around me and tried to imagine what he'd been doing all day — rushing on his short legs from one end of the house to the other, worrying first about the dogs, then about Linda — too small to get anything done.

He was gone a long time, and I had just gotten up to go after him when he came trudging in with a big metal dog dish half full of water. He was wet and frowning. "I couldn't find a pan," he said.

I took the dish, and without hesitating, slooshed the water into Meda's face.

"Run, Sonny," I yelled, dropping the dish and pushing him out the bedroom door and down the dark hallway. I herded him through the open front door, across the yard, and into a field of tall grass where we crouched, stiff and frightened, for some time. Eventually, Sonny turned over a rock and unearthed a whole colony of doodle bugs. By the time the cool evening breeze reached us and we spotted our mother's car coming up the road, we'd almost forgotten that we were hiding.

Linda was up by the time we went inside, dressed and sitting in her wheelchair. Meda was frying hamburger meat, and the indoor water dish was back on the rubber mat by the door.

Mother was waiting for us at the dining room table. "Did you have fun?" she asked.

* * *

Twice a month Daddy picked us up for the weekend. After pulling into the gravel drive and shutting off the engine, he'd sit motionless in his car — a long, pale green affair with curved fins like dragon wings — until he made up his mind to get out. I kept watch behind the living room blinds, and as soon as I saw his foot on the front steps, I'd run and wait behind the door. Once he rang the bell, I'd jerk the door open and throw myself into his arms. About this time,

Mother always wandered in. If we were on the porch, she'd say "Come in, George," and even as he was muttering something that meant no, he'd bend his head to come through the door. She'd stand with her arms across her chest, shifting from one foot to the other, making small talk and throwing me significant looks. She and I were both conspirators and rivals, and sometimes I went stiff with the confusion of it. I remember going for drives in that big station wagon of hers, Sonny and I in the backseat and Mother in front, so far away from us that we seemed to lose sight of her every time we crested a hill. She concocted stories on those drives about how life would be later, presumably when we all started living it again. Daddy was at the sunny center of all the stories. My brother and I began those drives feeling wary and resistant, but she had a way of chiding us into a state approaching her own: cheerful, even giddy. By the time we were four or five miles down the road, we'd be singing something from *South Pacific* or *The King and I*. For days after those rides, Sonny and I were like the dogs that kept their noses pressed to the fence, expecting every moment to be released.

Weekends with Daddy were always wonderful, no matter what we did. Back then, he was tall and thin with a nose like a small tomahawk. Arrogant but a little boyish too, he'd stand with his hands stuffed into his khaki pants, his flat top bristling with the electricity of his thoughts. I drank him in, trying to memorize his features so that I could call them back on nights when I couldn't sleep.

One Sunday night Daddy brought us home late, and to avoid Mother's anger, dropped us off in the driveway. We stood in the dark yard and watched him disappear in the dragon car before carrying our things to the front door. Both of us would have preferred to walk on down the road, arms full of dirty clothes, but Daddy had told us to slip quietly inside, and so we did. That night we were lucky. Mother was already asleep in the big double bed she and Sonny shared. "Be very quiet," I warned him. "Don't jiggle the bed when you get in."

Linda was waiting up for me, dressed in her nightgown but still in her chair. She was working a jigsaw puzzle by the light of the desk lamp. When I came up behind her I noticed first the clusters of pieces — aqua, pale blue, and tan — then the box propped against the wall and the picture of a tropical beach, a landscape so foreign to

Linda and me that it might as well have been on another planet. The sun was shining on the sand; it looked warm and peaceful.

Linda had a puzzle piece caught between her middle fingers, holding it aloft while she considered its place. Her hands weren't like mine or like anyone else's I'd ever seen. The fingers were long and thin, and instead of growing up in an orderly row as mine did, hers were bunched tightly together like the stalks of an emerging plant. I used to sit on the bed and squeeze my fingers together to see what it felt like to have hands like Linda's. Once, she'd caught me at it and shook her head.

"You don't want these old hands," she'd told me, and, of course, she was right.

When she had fit the piece into its slot, she twisted in her chair and gave me a close look. "You're shaking," she said with a frown. The skin between her eyes was bunched together like one of Meda's Pekingese. "Why are you so cold?"

"Well," I began, working the words from behind clenched teeth. "Sonny and I went to the fair with Daddy. We walked down the midway and fed the ducks."

"And you were cold the whole time?"

I nodded, remembering the chill that had wrapped itself around my bare legs.

"Why didn't you tell your dad?" she asked, swiveling her chair so she could face me.

It seemed to me she must know, but then I remembered Linda didn't have a father, that she'd told me she'd never had one. I couldn't imagine such a thing; it seemed the worst punishment of all. "Because I was afraid he would bring us home early," I finally said.

Linda didn't say anything, just reached for the spread on her bed. With some effort, she caught it between her fingers and held it out to me. "Wrap this around you," she said, and after I had finished, she motioned for me to press myself between the desk and her chair. "I need some help with my puzzle," she explained.

We worked together for maybe half an hour, and when I was warm and drowsy, I leaned back against her and fell into a sound sleep. Meda must have lifted both of us into bed that night. I woke the next morning with Linda's spread still wrapped tightly around me.

Meda loved her dogs, but she demonstrated care by taking care. I don't ever recall her playing with them. She watered and feed them; she cleaned their cages and spoke a few words while she went about her tasks.

After we'd been living with her a few months, she gave Sonny and me two tiny balls of mottled fur, Pekingese of course. They lived in a cage in the kitchen like guinea pigs, and when we took them out to play, we argued over which was which. Sonny's dog was named Fluffy.

"Here, Fluffy," he'd call. He expected his dog, whichever one it was, to come running at the sound of its name. Instead, both balls remained where they were, paralyzed by the large expanse of linoleum, the pairs of sneakers, and Sonny's pudgy hands waving and clapping encouragement. Clearly, all they wanted was to be rolled back into the cage.

"He doesn't know his name, stupid," I'd announce, hands on my hips. I hated calling Sonny names, but I did it anyway.

"He might," Sonny would counter, and though I'd shake my head and try to look disgusted, part of me wanted to believe him.

My dog went nameless. All the possibilities swam about in my head and confused me. Linda and I made lists and were narrowing the choices when Meda took the puppies back. She said Sonny and I weren't taking care of them. The next evening she sold them.

"Your mother is mean," I told Linda the night the puppies left. They were sold separately to families with small children. One of the little girls had pigtails and, watching the transaction from the window, I imagined jerking her hair and knocking her down. Sonny stayed in his room in the dark. Whenever someone hurt Sonny, he went them one better, mistreating himself to get revenge. He'd break his toys and stuff them into the wastebasket, choosing whatever was newest, brightest, best, a savage smile on his face. This time he curled up in a dark room and refused to eat.

"She does what she thinks she has to," Linda told me, her head bent over the puzzle pieces. This time she was putting together a misty photo of Big Ben. The name was printed in big red letters across the side of the box, and I read it over and over, trying to make sense of it. Big Ben sounded like the name of a lumberjack or a bear.

"She thinks she can do anything she wants to," I said bitterly. Linda didn't bother answering.

A few days later we were sitting at the dinner table when Meda leaned back in her chair, blew smoke into the air and announced, "I'm going after the dog."

I knew right away what she was talking about, but Mother didn't. She looked up from the sink, her face a question.

"What dog?" she asked.

"Down the road," Meda replied, her arm whipping through the air in the general direction. She puffed on her cigarette and stared out the window, her eyes narrowed against the smoke. Linda had already returned to her room.

"The one that's always tied up in his yard," I explained to Mother. "You know, the old house on the hill." But she didn't know, and she was surprised I did. Mother never expected Sonny or me to know anything she didn't.

The border collie was tethered outdoors, a constant sentry, regardless of the time of day or the season. The house he guarded had been built on a rise, really a hill by Texas standards, and open fields stretched away on three sides. Every time we drove by the dog was stationed at the edge of the yard, as far away as he could get from the stake that held him. Even from a distance, he looked ragged and filthy, and I wouldn't have known he was a collie if Meda hadn't told me, pointed him out as we passed, and added, "Person treating a dog like that oughta be shot." Just a few days before, Sonny and I had ridden with her to the grocery store, and on the way back, she'd pulled onto the shoulder and sat with the car idling, watching the dog watch her. It had been a cold, rainy day. The windshield wipers had swished back and forth on the glass; Sonny and I had sat silent in the back seat and waited. Once, he'd raised his finger to the window and opened his mouth to speak, but I'd pinched his leg and shook my head no. Glowering, he'd folded his arms across his chest and scooted to the other side of the seat.

"Is that a good idea?" my mother asked Meda. "Doesn't the dog belong to someone?"

"What belongs to you is what you take care of," Meda said. She ground out her cigarette in her plate, stood up, and walked out the door. Smoke curled and drifted up, reminding me of those signals Indians used to send. I wondered whether there were things I was missing, whether life would make more sense if I knew the codes. I studied what was left of the smoke until I heard the slam of the living room door; then, I went looking for Linda. Sonny was with her, sitting at the foot of her chair. He was trying to tie the strings of her booties together, but the big balls were getting in his way.

"Sonny, stop it," I ordered, but he went right on, his brown head bent to the task.

"It's all right," Linda said, brushing my arm with the ends of her fingers.

But it wasn't all right with me. "Leave Linda alone," I told him. When he didn't respond, I shoved him out of the way, and kneeled to straighten her shoes.

Neither of them wanted to talk to me, so to bring us back together I told them about Meda. Linda wheeled herself to the living room window and motioned for me to open the blinds. She looked pale and fragile sitting there, the thin evening light washing over her. I realized that in all the months I'd known her, Linda had never been outdoors. After a while I worried that she was cold and went to get her a blanket.

While I was in the bedroom, Meda returned. I heard the car stopping in the driveway, then someone yelling, and by the time I got to the living room, my mother was running out the door.

"Go see what's happening," Linda told me.

I went out on the porch and was drawn slowly down the walk toward the car. The air was alive with screaming and snarling, and when I reached the edge of the yard, I covered my ears with my hands and stood still. What I saw made no sense to me. The dog was everywhere, a blur of matted fur, biting both of them over and over again. Any child would have fought back or run away, but Mother and Meda did neither. After awhile, I realized Mother was trying to pull Meda away, but Meda wouldn't let go. Even as the dog tore into her skin, Meda tightened her grip.

"Keep back," my mother screamed at me, and I did as she said, sickened by the blood and the filmy terror in the dog's eyes. Eventually, he freed himself and scrambled over the hood of the car. His feet splayed out in all directions, and his toenails made screeching sounds on the metal. Even as he made a running leap toward home, his legs went on beating the air. When he was gone, Mother and Meda leaned against the car and turned their eyes on me. Meda held out her bloody arms like a prisoner waiting for handcuffs, and for a second she gave me another of those smiles, as though we shared some secret. Little pools of blood accumulated in the gravel around her feet. Mother sobbed and hugged her arms to her chest.

"Go get us some wet towels," Meda told me before sinking into the back seat of the car.

When I got back, Mother had propped herself in the driver's seat, and Meda was lying stretched across the back with her eyes closed. She opened them briefly to watch me wrap towels around her arms, but then she turned her head and closed them again. I looked away too and tried to hold my breath against the smell of so much blood. After I finished with Meda, I climbed over into the front seat and started again with Mother. Once, I had to go back inside for more towels, and I kept my head down so that Sonny and Linda couldn't see my face.

"We're fine, honey," my mother said as I crawled out of the car and slammed the doors shut. I could see Meda through the back window, her eyes closed, the white towels already soaked through with blood. She looked as though she might be dying. I remember the crunch of gravel under the tires as my mother backed slowly out the drive and, when they were gone, the heavy weight of my fear. I didn't tell Linda how bad it had looked to me, though I desperately wanted to, but she must have known because she sat waiting all those hours by the window.

* * *

We moved a few weeks later, and I never saw Meda or Linda again. Mother remarried not long afterwards and had three daughters in three years. Daddy remarried, too. His new wife already had a boy the same age as Sonny, and she soon got pregnant and bore my father another daughter. Sonny and I were part of both families, but somehow not at the center of either. It took a long time, but we grew up and had families of our own.

Mother came to visit mine just this past Thanksgiving. We were driving down the highway to the shopping mall one afternoon, my two beautiful sons strapped into the back, when I happened to mention Linda. I don't remember why.

"You're always thinking about Linda," my mother said. She was looking out the window at the winter fields. Maybe she was remembering her childhood in Missouri, the fields her father sharecropped.

"I just wish I knew what happened to her," I said. Meda had been dead for a long time. Only a few years after we moved away she'd killed herself. Somehow, my mother had learned of her death, and for her own reasons, had passed the news on to me. Ever since then, for more than twenty-five years, I'd been wondering about Linda, who had no father, no other family or friends.

"Well," Mother replied, pulling her gaze from the fields to the highway in front of us, "I think she got married, didn't she?"

I said nothing at all, but something terrible was happening to my heart. People see what they want to see, I told myself, remember what they want to remember. Hadn't I known it all along? In the back seat my baby son was babbling, trying out his voice on a few notes, the beginning of a song. Mother shifted in her seat to listen; a sad smile lingered on her face. I kept my hands steady on the wheel and my eyes on the road, but somewhere inside I was swerving, first toward and then away.

Christina's World

"The way this tempera happened, I was
in an upstairs room in the Olson house and saw
Christina crawling in the field."
— Andrew Wyeth

I. 1930

Christina enjoyed watching the girls' hands as they fingered the shells — picking them up, turning them over slowly, putting them down again — always cautious, as though they couldn't trust their hands to do their bidding. These were well-mannered little girls whose mothers had taught them to safeguard the possessions of others, and so they were cautious, though there was no real need to be. Plump and steady with palms pink and soft as kittens' paws, the small hands held the shells to ears, to the light, and out to Christina. She declined them. Her own hands had dropped so many shells she didn't dare pick them up anymore. Not that the shells were valuable, though some were rare enough in this part of the world, but they were a legacy of sorts, something to remind generations to come that theirs had once been a sea-faring family. Besides, Christina didn't like for the girls to see that her own fingers were stiff as winter twigs. While she didn't pretend that she could walk or do things she couldn't, she did stay put when the girls came to visit. If they wanted something to eat or drink, she let them rummage about for themselves. Children crave trust, and she gave it to them.

The girl named Betsy was Christina's favorite. Dark eyed and somber, Betsy loved the color blue and wore it nearly every day. Her dresses were starched stiff and shiny, the deep blue of forget-me-nots or the soft blue of the summer sky. In navy, with a white linen collar, she looked pale and a little somber. Christina tried not to favor, but, to her, children were like cats, some easier to love than others. If Betsy had been a cat, she would have been the sort to curl up in Christina's lap and go off to sleep, a warm pulsing ball of fur.

But she was a girl, so she sat cross-legged on the floor near Christina's chair, fingering the nautilus that rested in the pouch her dress made. In the fading afternoon light, the blue of Betsy's dress became a pool for the nautilus. Christina narrowed her eyes and imagined she saw the shell drift. The room was so quiet she could hear the ins and outs of Betsy's breath. The other little girl was across the room, busying herself with arranging long lines of shells. Christina watched her for a moment, then turned back to Betsy, reaching out with one thin hand to touch the top of the child's head. Betsy's hair was warm where the sun had been shining on it and soft. Each year it grew longer and smoother. The first summer she'd spent in Cushing, Betsy had been eight, her hair short and snug, like a cap. Right away, she'd been drawn to the loose knot of hair at Christina's nape. Only a few weeks after they'd met, the little girl began coming over in the late evenings to comb it. Betsy wanted her own long hair, but her mother said no, not until she was old enough to care for it herself. Combing and braiding Christina's hair served as practice.

Coarse and a little uneven, Christina's hair fell to her waist, and when it was left hanging, looked for all the world like God's leftovers — red, black, gray, blonde — all sewn onto one poor head. Betsy thought it was the most beautiful hair in the world, and every evening she combed, braided, and unbraided, twisting the long straight strands around her sturdy fingers in a vain effort to curl them. Christina sat very still during these sessions, a little bird of happiness in her throat. Sometimes Betsy pulled the hair so tight that Christina's temples pulsed with blood, but she was careful never to betray any discomfort. Often, Betsy's fingers would stray across the back of

Christina's neck, and when this happened, memories of Christina's mother would rise like vapors in the room.

Her mother had been dead for a year, but her ghost did not pass easily. At thirty-seven, Christina was still more her mother's daughter than she was anything else, so she resisted letting go. This room, this museum to the sea, had been her mother's creation. The shell picture frames, coated with dust now, had been hers. She had hung the lace curtains in the window and made sure every visitor got the grand tour. Often, during the summer, more visitors than family had lived in the house. Now it was only Christina and Alvaro and their father in this huge house meant to hold so many more.

Kate Hathorne Olson had been the artistic sort. Christina remembered all the hours her mother had devoted to making the little shell table, whole days spent kneeling on the floor, surrounded by old newsprint, bottles of glue, and piles and piles of tiny shells. One by one, she'd stuck them on, covering then recovering, until the table was so thoroughly encrusted it appeared to have been made entirely of shells. Since then, Christina had heard several people call it tacky. Once, Fred's wife had wondered aloud why anyone would want such a useless table, but, for Christina, these comments missed the point. Unlike the rest of them, her mother had left something behind besides children. Hands folded in her lap, Christina looked away from the table and wondered what she might leave for others, certainly not tables or children, perhaps nothing at all.

Betsy's friend wandered about the room, her hands clasped behind her back, as though she'd decided not to touch another thing and was going to make sure her hands didn't try any tricks. Christina knew the girl would soon say that it was time to go, and then Betsy, always obliging, would stand and return the nautilus to its place before saying good bye. Once the girls left, the house would be unnaturally still, and Christina would feel the chill that came when those she loved had just closed her door.

"Do you like stories about witches?" Christina asked loudly in the girl's direction. "Did Betsy ever tell you about my ancestor, John Hathorne? He was the chief judge at the witch trials in Salem."

"Witches?" The girl turned to Christina but avoided meeting her eyes. Round, white and blank, the girl's face was like a fancy china plate, pretty but empty. Christina couldn't help not liking her very much. "Do you believe in witches?" the girl asked before adding, "My momma says there's no such thing."

"Your momma's right, dear," Christina replied. "Most people to-day know better than to believe in witches, but back in 1692 lots of folks believed in them, especially the folks in Salem."

"We learned about it in school," Betsy said, nodding her head importantly.

"We did too," the girl agreed quickly, her hand edging across the table until it seized a shiny purple shell, shaped like a clam. She closed her fist around it. The shell was one of Christina's favorites, and she sighed, wishing the girl hadn't chosen it.

"The whole thing began innocently enough, just a group of bored girls wanting to know whether the future held anything in store for them." Christina paused, then, seeing that she had girls' attention, went on. "They wanted to find out whether they would get married and have children, whether they had any happy gay times to look forward to. Salem was a cold and solemn place, you see. Seems there was this servant who could tell fortunes from looking at tea leaves in the bottom of a cup."

"Really?" Betsy asked, her face so open that Christina knew she would have been the first to believe.

"There's no telling if it was true, but the girls believed in it because the servant told them happy things they wanted to hear. Whatever sad things she saw in those leaves she must have kept to herself." Christina smiled, thinking she told a good story. "Sooner or later, though, they were bound to be caught at their mischief, and, wouldn't you know it, the preacher himself discovered them." Christina shook her head. "Oh, it was an awful time in Salem. To keep from being punished for doing something their parents saw as the devil's mischief, the girls said they'd been enchanted..."

"What's enchanted mean?" Betsy's friend asked.

"Under a spell. The girls said others had been making them do these things. It wasn't true, of course, but the frightened girls might well have believed it. They didn't set out to hurt anyone, and neither did my ancestor John Hathorne, but many innocent lives were destroyed. Those who were responsible had to pay, their families, too, and those who came so much later, born far from Salem, were still somehow doing penance."

Betsy looked bewildered, and Christina regretted her words. The child would never understand, not even if Christina could have explained. Two hundred years had elapsed between the trials of Salem and the birth of Christina Olson. To claim a connection was more than silly; it was the same sort of nonsensical thinking that had brought about the trials in the first place. Still, the feelings persisted.

"Did I ever tell you about Samuel Sewall, Betsy?" Christina asked.

The girl shook her dark head. Christina watched Betsy's friend return the purple shell to the window ledge and move over to sit down beside them. She'd obviously forgotten her intention to leave. Looking down into their faces, so wide-eyed and expectant, Christina knew exactly how the whole problem in Salem had come about. No one is more open to suggestion than a young girl with hormones racing through her blood and the nubs of breasts rubbing against the starched front of her dress. Everything becomes at once possible, delightful, and frightening. The whole world reflects the mystery taking place in her body, a mystery no one bothers to explain. Was it any wonder those girls in Salem huddled together and read tea leaves to discover the future? The present was a closed box they were desperate to break out of.

"Samuel Sewall was a chief juror in the witch trials," she said, looking away from their glowing eyes to the window and what she could see of the darkening sea. The waves were gathering strength, swelling as they approached land, then flattening themselves on the shore. If she stared too long, she knew the house would begin to rock like a hapless ship at sea. Pulling her eyes away, she trained them again on Betsy and her friend, who was sniffing at the air, as though something in the kitchen were burning or would be soon.

The girl is determined to keep me off balance, Christina thought. With a sinking heart, she launched into the rest of her story. "After the girls' hysteria had run its course and the hangings had stopped, sanity came creeping back to Salem, and the people who'd taken part in condemning the innocent were filled with the most horrible remorse. Samuel Sewall was stricken worse than the rest, though only God knows why. I'm sure my ancestor John Hathorne must have suffered too, but certainly not nearly so much as Mr. Sewall. The poor man had fourteen healthy children when the trials began, but as soon as they ended, a horrible plague descended on his family. One by one his children were taken from him. A son fell to smallpox then a daughter, too. The next year his youngest boy was thrown under the wheels of a wagon, and Mr. Sewall had only just buried him when another daughter, not much more than a child herself, died in childbirth. And if that wasn't enough misery, the same summer Mr. Sewall's eldest son was shot under mysterious circumstances." She paused, weighing whether or not they were old enough to be told that a woman was involved, a married woman at that, decided that they weren't and went on.

"Mr. Sewall had lost more than most of us ever lose in a lifetime, but he still had a family to gather round him when his youngest son was lost in a blizzard and froze to death. Poor wandering soul. I think of him when the whole world outside is white and the wind is beating against the walls of this old house, trying to get in. One of the blessings of not being able to walk is that I'm bound to die right here in my own house." Christina's voice faded away, and all three pairs of eyes were drawn to the window. Outside, the sky was streaked with purple, a summer sky, but beneath it they imagined a boy wandering lost in a world of white. Christina felt guilty for telling them such a sad story. She knew she shouldn't before she began, but she couldn't stop. They deserved better, but hadn't Samuel Sewall's children deserved better, too? None of it made sense. There was no lesson to be learned, so why burden the children with it? In fact she could no longer remember who had told her about Sewall and his children. Perhaps she'd even dreamed it. Sometimes she had the strangest dreams. Still, in her heart, she knew it was as good as truth, wherever it had come from, and that once she had started, she had to finish it.

"Eventually," she said, pretending interest in the sunset, "they were all gone, poor darlings, all fourteen children and his wife, too. It was Mr. Sewall's misery to watch his entire family die."

"But why?" Betsy asked. Her friend was tracing her name on the dusty floor, no longer listening.

Christina only smiled at Betsy and shook her head, as if she didn't know.

II. 1935

On the first of November, Christina woke early, even before the light that rose like a mist around the house, coloring the world around them in shades of gold, and green, and gray. Usually, she slept for several hours after dawn, but on this morning she woke in the dark, so chilled she wanted only to get into the kitchen by the stove. Later, she realized her waking had been more than chance. Not that she'd known what Al intended to do, but she had noticed the restlessness in his body when he'd come through the front hallway the night before, stood in the half-light so she couldn't see his eyes or mouth, and asked, "Are you certain you don't want it, Anna?" She was certain.

He only called her Anna when he meant to be formal or distant, and last night he'd meant to be both. Since their father's funeral he'd been keeping to himself, going up and down the stairs, in and out of the rooms on the second and third floors, pulling doors closed behind him with final-sounding clicks. He seemed to be looking for something, but she knew he'd never find it in the house. What he'd lost had been gone so long she doubted he remembered what it felt like. Al was a tethered animal on a long leash, and Christina was the stake that held him.

For the last fifteen years, he'd had the both of them to care for, their father crippled with arthritis and Christina by polio. The two of them had been reason enough for Al to give up fishing for farming, to spend his days hauling wood and cutting hay, but now that Al had lifted his father from his wheelchair into his casket, she alone would be keeping him from the sea.

Since childhood, she'd trained herself against wondering what might have been: the doctors in Boston had told her she'd never get better and she'd had the sense to believe them. What had become of that sense now? For ten nights, ever since their father's funeral, Christina had been having the same dream, a dream in which she was completely, remarkably well. She woke each morning to a damp pillowcase and got up early to escape it. During the day, she kept her eyes from Al's, afraid that if she caught his glance, she'd know for certain what he was feeling. He roamed the house and the fields, and she watched him go, his slender, already stooped figure, going up the stairs and out the door.

"I'll be going out now," he told her on the morning of the eleventh day.

She was still making her way to her chair, and she never spoke until she was situated. The exertion left her breathless, and once she'd hoisted herself into her chair, it was several minutes before she could speak without panting. Al always busied himself with something until she was ready to talk.

"Breakfast?" she asked.

"Had a little bread and some coffee an hour ago, thank you." He was looking out the window at the season's first snowfall.

Ten days ago, when they'd made their way from the house to the family graveyard down the hill, the ground had been dry, even dusty. Christina had conceded to ride in her father's wheelchair, and she remembered the dirt rising in small clouds around the turning wheels. On the way down, it had seemed more like autumn than winter, but as she'd sat at the grave site, listening to the swell of the preacher's voice, she'd felt the bite of wind from the north, wind so damp and chilly it was bound to bring snow. Even she, housebound most her life, knew a winter wind when she felt it. Shivering, the sharp bones of her elbows knocking against the metal arms of the chair, she'd tried to deny the joy she felt at being out-of-doors. The wind tugged at her hair, pulling it free of the neat bun one of the sister-in-laws had fashioned for her. Christina felt chill bumps rising on the skin of her arms and legs, and she sighed deeply out of happiness. The low drone of the preacher's voice brought her back for a time, but she couldn't bear to waste these precious moments mourning her father. She'd have the rest of her life for that and, besides, he was out to sea now. Turning her face south to the bay, she opened her mouth to the damp salt air. How happy he must be, she thought. Afterwards, Christina sat alone in her chair at the table and felt the sea air drying her skin, pulling it taut. And that night she'd had the dream for the first time.

Al went on standing at the window. He was waiting for her to say something, but they'd always kept their secrets, and she thought it best they go on keeping them. "Looks like we could get several more inches of snow," she offered, and when he didn't respond, she pulled the white cloth from the dishes on the table and draped it across a chair. If Al had been thinking of her, he'd have brought her a cup of coffee, but his mind was out to sea.

She waited, thinking he might turn and leave, but when he didn't, she hitched her chair across the floor to the stove, taking care not to put more strain on the chair's legs than she had to. Christina knew she was foolish to refuse the wheelchair, but everyone was granted a certain amount of foolishness, weren't they?

By the time she'd poured her coffee and drank enough of it so she could inch back across the floor without slopping, Al had left the window. She heard him in the front hallway, knocking about and pushing the chair this way and that. It had a squeak no amount of oil would silence. While their father was alive, Christina had learned to ignore it, or rather to incorporate it into the small group of sounds she associated with her father: sudden yells and snorts; the gentle wheeze that signaled he'd fallen asleep in the chair; that deep, despondent laugh; and the squeak, squeak, squeak of his chair. Now that the other sounds were gone, the squeak was an affront to her. She was relieved when Al opened the front door and pushed the chair outside. The door slammed, and her cup rattled in its saucer. She picked it up and took another sip. A moment later, she saw him from the window as he came around the side of the house, pushing the chair in front of him. He looked so strange. Passersby, seeing him from the road, would probably assume he'd lost his senses. Briefly, she wondered herself but pushed that thought aside and went on with her coffee. He didn't so much as glance in at her. His eyes were on what lay ahead. She fixed hers on the tracks he was leaving. Children might have danced between them.

Four times each year, Christina got out of bed, made her way to the window, and looked out to find children playing in the fields. In winter, they rolled huge balls of snow and hauled sleds up the hill. In spring, they threw balls and wove garlands of flowers. They appeared only once each season, and this regularity reassured Christina, who knew they weren't real. Years ago, when they first began coming, she'd called Al to the window without telling him why. "Look out there," she told him. He'd obliged then turned back at her with a puzzled smile. "What is it?" he'd asked. Disappointed, she sent him on his way. After a while, she stopped wishing she could share them and came to regard them as the children who should have been: her mother's brothers and sisters, her own children and Alvaro's.

Though the fresh snow and frigid air portended a new season, the children stayed away. Maybe it was her father, newly buried, that kept them from coming or maybe it was wild-eyed Alvaro, pushing the empty wheelchair God knows where. But the children would have to come soon. She could see her breath in the kitchen. Surely that meant the end of fall, no matter what the calendar said.

In winter, the house was nearly as cold as the outdoors. The man who occasionally helped them cut wood had once remarked that heating the Olson place was like heating a lobster trap, and Christina supposed he wasn't far from wrong. To conserve heat, they closed off the second and third floors. Some of the panes in the upstairs windows were broken, and these Alvaro had stuffed with balls of rags the size of someone's head. Even so, the wind found its way through. Because Christina fretted and felt guilty, Al never told her about the broken panes. But, the summer before, when he'd carried her out to see the flowers, she'd glanced up and caught sight of one of the rag balls. Abruptly, she'd screamed, and, startled, Al had dropped her. The pain was sickening, and for days she worried she'd broken her hip. After that, she was confined to the house. Al no longer offered to carry her outdoors, and she no longer asked.

He was halfway to the shore before Christina realized he meant to shove the wheelchair into the water. "What's gotten into him?" she asked herself, her eyes on the small brown spot moving steadily away. Eventually, she leaned forward, knocking the dishes to the floor. Something broke, but Christina didn't look to see. Al was at the water's edge by then, about to shove the chair in. But he didn't just push it in. He stood at the end of the dock, lifted the chair over his head, and heaved it out to sea. When it hit, water splashed back, drenching him, but he continued to stand there, stupidly watching the chair bob on the surface then slowly sink. "Come back you old fool," Christina yelled, banging feebly on the glass. He didn't hear her, of course, and she could do nothing except wait for him to return. When he got inside his coat and pants were no longer wet; they were frozen.

"Take off your clothes and stand by the stove," she begged him, hitching off in the chair for a blanket, but by the time she got back, he'd gone to his room and closed the door. Al lay in bed for two days, but on the third day, when Christina was on the verge of panic, he got up and asked her for a cup of coffee. Neither of them mentioned the wheelchair, but Christina often thought of it. Had it stayed in the spot where it sank or did the currents carry it off to sea?

III. 1939

Betsy had grown up. Though Christina had no idea when it had happened or why she hadn't noticed before, the Betsy standing in front of her was no longer a girl. And if that weren't enough, she'd brought a strange young man with her, too. Christina sat heavily in her chair and could think of nothing to say.

Ever since Betsy was a girl, she and her family had spent their summers in Maine. Each year she appeared on their doorstop after a nine months' absence, and Al and Christina were shocked. The child standing patiently on the step, waiting to be asked in, was never the Betsy they remembered. She'd be taller; her hair would be longer or sometimes shorter. The roundness of her childish face would have given way a little more, but after she stepped over the threshold and dropped into Al's rocking chair, she would become suddenly herself again, no different really than the year before.

Christina recalled those other summers clearly. June evenings in Maine were still cool enough for sweaters, and Betsy's mother always sent her daughter off with one draped over her shoulders. More absentminded than dutiful, Betsy left her sweater exactly as her mother had arranged it on the walk over, but once inside the house, she'd shrug it off onto the table or the nearest chair. Most often, it slipped to the floor and a cat curled up in it. When the visit was over, Christina stooped from her chair to retrieve it. She'd brush the sweater thoroughly, and replace it on Betsy's shoulders with strict instructions to walk quickly home. In this way, Christina had hoped to convey to Betsy's mother the love she felt for her child.

Today, Betsy wasn't wearing a sweater. The unfairness of it welled

32

up in Christina so that she had to turn her face away. Just when Betsy's family had seen fit to buy a farmhouse up the road and move to Maine on a year-round basis, Betsy had gone and turned into a young woman. Christina would still love her, of course, but adults and children were as different as dogs and cats. People had their preferences, and hers were for cats and children. Children knew how to relax and be natural around her. They didn't have to pretend that she was like everybody else because they usually didn't notice she was any different. Adults and dogs tried too hard to be friendly and made everyone uncomfortable in the process.

Christina had to admit that the young man Betsy had brought with her was an exception. He didn't seem to be trying at all, and in fact acted as though he were sitting down with family or close friends, which was all the more odd since Christina knew he'd only just met Betsy as well. His name was Andy, and he was all eyebrows and nose and wide grin. Al was smiling too, and Christina supposed she should at least be pleased for her brother. He so loved a bit of company, no matter who it was. Christina decided she should try to forgive Betsy for bringing this scarecrow of a man. After all, growing up wasn't her fault.

"I'm going out for a pipe," Al said, grabbing his cap and ducking his head to Andy. "Care to come?"

Christina smiled at Al. She knew he wanted both the smoke and the company, but he wanted the company more. If Andy didn't agree to join him, Al would go out on the porch and smoke alone, but he'd be wishing the whole time he were back inside where the talk was. He'd puff and puff and make himself sick to be done with a bowl full. On the other hand, if Andy were to sit out with him, he'd nurse that same bowl until dusk.

Andy didn't seem to have heard the invitation. He was standing with his back to them stroking the wall, which was nothing more than bare planks. Christina thought of telling him to watch out or he'd have a hand full of splinters, but part of her was hoping he'd get himself a few.

Just when they thought he'd forgotten all about them, Andy said, "Be glad to, Al." Then he said something surprising. "Mind if I do a few sketches of the house?" Turning, he shone his wide grin on the whole room. "I don't know how it happens, but some houses end up with more character than a whole roomful of people. There's so much to learn from a house like this." He shrugged and seemed embarrassed for having made a speech. Christina looked closely at him.

"Help yourself," she said. "And watch out for splinters on those walls."

When the men were gone, Christina and Betsy sat quietly, listening to the squeaks of the porch and the drone of the voices outside. Al seemed to be explaining something.

"Still going off to college, are you?" Christina finally asked.

"Oh, yes," Betsy replied, nodding repeatedly. "It's all I ever think about."

"Well, it's a wonderful opportunity," Christina said, knowing that it was but wishing all the same that Betsy wouldn't take it. "I don't hear them talking out there, do you? Where do you suppose they've gone?"

Betsy got up and peered out the window, then laughed and motioned for Christina. "Come look," she said.

Sighing for show, Christina hitched her chair over to where she could see out. Al was nowhere around, but Andy was perched on the roof of his car, his legs crossed Indian-style, a sketchbook in his lap.

"He's an odd one," Christina said, thinking how like a cat it was to climb up on something to gain a vantage point. Dogs never thought to do things like that.

"He told me this morning he's in pre-med at the University of Pennsylvania," Betsy said in a voice Christina had never heard. But when she trailed her hand across Christina's shoulder, the touch was so casual and warm that Christina was reassured. Maybe she would get used to this new Betsy.

"Phooey," Christina snorted and reached up to pat her hand. "You've got to stop believing everything you're told."

IV. 1948

One summer morning Christina looked out the window and saw bumblebees burrowing in her flowers, silly creatures buried up to their wings with only the fat tips of their bottoms showing. They looked so ridiculous with their round yellow and black bodies and those tiny transparent wings. Who would imagine they could fly? When one buzzed in the open window she couldn't bring herself to be frightened and shooed it away with the back of her hand. Offended, the bee stung; almost immediately, a knot the size of a thimble rose on her wrist. Christina pressed a cold cloth to it, and when Al came in from lunch she hid it from him. He'd just fret about screens for the windows, something they couldn't afford. Besides, Christina liked being able to stick her arm out whenever she wanted to feel the outdoors, and the open windows allowed the cats to come and go as they pleased.

For the cats, going out was considerably easier than coming in. The windows were too high off the ground for the cats to leap through. Instead, they had to jump and grab with their front claws for the window ledge, then scramble up the side of the house with their back legs, scraping and scratching away whatever paint was left. Christina liked to witness the instant they gained control and made the leap inside. Always, their expressions turned serene, even haughty. She appreciated that about them: they could immediately forget the struggle.

Sometimes at night, Christina would lie on her pallet downstairs and imagine she was a cat prowling in and out of the upstairs rooms, many of which had been closed off so long she could no longer remember what they contained. Probably, they were only bare and dusty, but she liked to think of curling her sleek cat body around dark heavy furniture before leaping onto a thick, soft mattress. She believed cats were God's most fortunate creatures: fearless, graceful, and completely independent.

Lately, a porcupine had taken to visiting, too, though obviously not through the window. On nice evenings, Al left the kitchen door open, and one night a fat little porcupine found his way inside. Lumbering across the room, he headed for the pantry, ate his fill of whatever had been dropped on the floor, then wandered back out again. "Well, I'll be," Al had said that first night. "Looks like the animals aren't going to wait until the house falls down to start rummaging around in it."

Christina looked forward to the porcupine's visits and took to dropping more than her share of food on the pantry floor to make sure he returned often. Once, she dreamed she touched him, and the quills weren't at all as she had imagined them to be. Not rough and prickly but smooth and polished, like hard wood toothpicks. In her dream, the porcupine sat on her lap, his quills back, so she could stroke them. On awakening, she had the sensation of accomplishing something new, and she lay very still to hold onto the pleasure she felt. Finally, opening her eyes, Christina stared at the ceiling, dark slabs of wood nobody had ever bothered to paint. In the half-light, the wood looked so waterlogged and heavy that she rolled out of bed and crawled as quickly as she could to the door. She'd decided then to go outside and see the house for herself.

A week passed before she could gather her energy and quiet her nerves. She left the house rarely and never alone. In preparation, she surveyed all the first floor windows to decide which way to go. The front of the house faced the road and the back, the sea. Either way, she was likely to be noticed. The alternative was to go, instead, toward the family graveyard, off to one side of the house. That direction, too, led to the sea, but she had no intention of dragging herself so far. All she wanted was to get to the wild blueberries, and if Al happened to see her, she could tell him she'd come out to see how the crop was doing. Not that he would require an explanation, but she would give him one to keep the air clean between them.

The hardest part was getting out the door. The porch steps had all but rotted away, and the drop from the porch to the ground was sizeable. Christina felt like one of the cats struggling to pull its hind legs onto the window sill. She had to slide slowly and carefully out the door and off the porch to keep her legs from being rubbed raw.

By the time she'd pulled herself to the edge of the yard, she was gasping for breath. Frightened by the pounding of her heart and the rattling of her lungs, she lay back on the ground to rest. As she grew still, the air came alive with smells both familiar and strange: grass, ripening berries, the sea, and something else she couldn't put a name to.

After a while the lumpy ground beneath her hips and the burning of her palms ceased to trouble her, and Christina opened her eyes to the field that stretched out around her. The witch grass and goldenrod bent in waves, swishing as the wind moved through, then moaning as it returned. Everything made noise, even if it was only a stirring, because everything was alive. She was alive too, making little grunting sounds as she moved. She pushed forward slowly — first stretching out one arm, then scooting with her hip — rather like the caterpillars that inched among her flowers. The wind loosened her hair, so that it, too, was swept from side to side and sometimes into her mouth. Nothing mattered now; she had never felt stronger.

Once, she stopped and put her head to the ground, listening to the silence of the earth with one ear and the whirring of the cicadas overhead with the other. She remembered how the boys used to pitch tents in the oak grove beyond the house. Girls got to stay until dark; then they walked slowly home together, chittering and twirling in the grass. The noise of the cicadas was all around; they felt the nervous intensity of insects in their bloodstreams. Though she limped and had to walk slowly, Christina had been much like the other girls then. None of them ever wondered where they came from but only where they would go. She recalled they'd all expected to go somewhere.

When she'd dragged herself the necessary distance, Christina fished in her pocket for a photograph taken of the family in 1900. She'd been seven years old and so proud of her dress. Her mother had spent the morning hooking and tying and wet combing before pushing the family out the door and instructing them to stand together in front of the house. In 1900, it had been a different house, just as they'd been different people. Painted white, with tall pines growing behind it, the structure had loomed large and proud, dwarfing the family so that those who saw the photograph never noticed Christina's frilly dress or Al's combed hair. The house was what was important to preserve for history, the real living entity in the picture.

And after forty-eight years would it still be so, Christina wondered. Her heart pounded when she opened her eyes, not from exertion but from fear. Her whole life had been spent inside this house, and like the soul which doesn't understand the weaknesses of the body it inhabits, Christina expected the house to endure, to be there even when she and Al were gone. Recently, she'd begun to worry that it wouldn't be, that the whole structure would cave in, even while she and Al were still living, that they'd have to crawl out of the rubble, like rats. She wanted to leave something behind, if not children or tables then at least this house.

Stretching toward it, Christina opened her eyes. The house looked smaller from this distance and fragile, too. The white paint had worn completely away, and the pine trees had disappeared, though she couldn't remember what had become of them. Perhaps they'd gone for fire wood. The siding had weathered to a sad and ghostly-looking gray. In its heyday, as the Hathorne house, this place had been home to a continual round of parties and weddings and births. Now it was home to Christina and Al, a humbler lot who expected little more of the house or themselves than that they endure. And she could see that the house had endured and would go on, shabby or no, without her.

Relieved, she turned her attention to the waning of the day, to the sounds in the grass and the smells in the air. She could be proud of this one thing at least: she took very little for granted. Once, Christina thought she saw a face in one of the upstairs windows. Was Andy were up there painting again, she wondered. He didn't knock anymore. Like the porcupine, he just lumbered in and found what he needed. For all she knew, he might have been working upstairs all day. After a time, Christina forgot about Andy and even about Al and the house. She lay back and enjoyed the warmth of the sun and the breeze that brushed her face and neck with the dampness of the sea.

Strangers

On the way out the door — she was pushing Jules and he was twisting around, trying to ask where they were going — she happened to glance at the far wall and see a huge silverfish skittering across the empty space where she'd never hung a picture. Naturally, her first thought was to run back in and swat the damn thing, but she didn't have time. They were late already and would have to walk fast down the hill.

Jules stared up at her while she locked the door, but Marsha kept her eyes away from his. On the walk across the parking lot, she made a point of studying the wall of apartment buildings to their left. Last-minute leavers were hurrying out, jumping in their cars, and roaring away. Marsha grabbed Jules's hand. It felt cool and small, and she was aware that if she squeezed too hard she could hurt him. Thoughts like this one came to her more often now, and she worried about what they meant.

Just as she expected, his steps slowed as they approached the hill; then, he began to drag and she to pull, his tennis shoes a reluctant scuff-scuff against the click-click of her heels. She was so certain of his resistance that when she finally heard him say, "No, Momma," she didn't know whether she'd heard Jules's voice or the one in her head. At odd moments, while eating lunch at her desk or in the midst of a dream, his little, breathless voice would startle her, sometimes whole sentences, but mostly just, "No, Momma," like now.

Forcing a smile, Marsha looked down at him and tried to imagine being one of those mothers she used to see on situation comedies when she was growing up. What would Donna Reed say? It was pathetic really; Donna Reed would never be in this situation.

"It's okay, Jules. Everyone's scared at first, but we all went to school. That's the way it is. I went, Daddy went, even Grandma and Grand-dad went. You'll like it after a while, I promise."

Lame, she thought, very lame, but her words seemed to keep him moving, so she went on talking, saying whatever came to mind — soft, soothing, motherly words. All the while, she thought of that silverfish on the wall, the way its back slapped back and forth like an excited puppy's. She was keeping it firmly in mind, following its movements in her head. Later, when Jules was safely on the bus, she'd go home briefly, expose the insect — under a potholder or wherever — and smash it.

Jules was quiet, his arm limp as she dragged him along. Now, he refused to meet her eyes. When she looked down, she saw the top of his dark head, so small and fragile looking. By the time they stepped onto the grass, the bus was already waiting at the bottom of the hill. She heard the heavy rattle-rattle of the engine — the same sound she remembered from childhood — and the murmur of children standing in a long, wavering line to get on. On Monday, Marsha had been startled at the number of children, twenty or more. She'd rarely seen kids playing outside the complex. They must all stay inside, she thought, feeling sorry for them. The line was orderly but slow, and cars piled up behind the yellow bus for blocks.

For the third day in a row, Jules was the last child in line and the only one shrieking and crying. Of course, the other children stared, their faces impassive, more like adults' faces than children's. The first morning, Marsha tried to shame him by pointing to others, some even smaller and more vulnerable looking than he, but Jules would have none of it. He clung to her and moaned, "Please don't make me." Prying his fingers from her arm, Marsha had felt a small but important part of her going numb.

As the line dwindled, Jules began to resist in earnest. Yanking his hand from hers, nearly falling on the damp, slick grass, he turned and ran toward the apartment. This was something new. Yesterday and the day before he'd merely screamed and pleaded. Surprised, Marsha could only yell out, "Stop, right now," and marvel at how he'd known instinctively to change his tactics. She'd shored herself up against screaming and begging, but she wasn't dressed to run. Jules kept going, but when he reached the edge of the parking lot, Marsha, thinking of cars, chased after him. Lunging for him, she turned her foot and the heel of her shoe cracked. Her ankle scraped against the pavement, and one run, then two, went zipping up her leg; she could feel them, a pair of tiny insects skittering up her calf and thigh.

"Damn you," Marsha cried out. "How much more do you think I can take?"

Jules looked up at her, his eyes wild like his father's and timid like her own. They were brown eyes flecked with gold, not her color or Craig's. Seeing how frightened he was made her want to cry.

"We've got to hurry now," Marsha told him. She hated it that she'd passed on to him the thing she most disliked in herself—that shrinking back from whatever was difficult or painful.

Hurriedly, she stepped out of her shoes and bent over to gather them up. But Jules wanted to help now. "Here, Momma," he said, grabbing one shoe and thrusting it into her hand.

"Let's run, Jules." She reached for his hand, and he grasped hers quickly. Always, he was frightened of losing her, but especially since his father had been gone.

Her purse banged against her thigh as she ran, and when they leaped the curb of the parking lot, Marsha stubbed her toe and dropped a shoe. Jules wanted to turn back for it, but she jerked him ahead.

"Never mind, Jules. I'll get it on the way back."

He was happy running downhill on the wet grass. She could see his pleasure in the way he bit his lower lip and waved his free hand. At play with Momma, she thought. She felt almost happy herself until she saw the last child was boarding.

"Wait," she cried out, waving, too. "There's one more!" Jules yelled along with her, his voice screechy and out of breath.

Cars were backed up all the way down the street. She could see the faces of the drivers. Of course they were watching. What else was there for them to do? She knew how ridiculous she must look, running downhill in her straight black skirt, a shoe in one hand and a reluctant son in tow.

41

Still, Marsha thanked God the bus driver had waited; she thought the momentum was going to carry her through. Then, they reached the open door and the steps, and, for Jules, the game was over. He drew up short and began screaming in that piercing way he had. "No, Momma, no. I can't. I can't."

Marsha tried forcing him to climb the stairs, but he flailed and kicked. Finally, she picked him up and dragged him on board. The bus driver, a middle-aged woman, stared openly. Marsha knew exactly what she was thinking, how pathetic it was that some women had children at all. Tonight, she'd describe the scene at the dinner table, Marsha struggling with her hysterical son. She was on the verge of screaming herself. Everyone waited for her to take control, but she didn't know how.

"All right, Jules," she gasped. "I give up."

Letting go of him, she backed off the bus; he scrambled up and followed. As they climbed the hill, she heard the roar of the bus taking off, then the zoom of cars unclotting and following. Jules trudged silently behind. Marsha unlocked the front door and let him in. The silverfish hadn't moved. She walked past it, into the bedroom to call in sick for the third day in a row. When she came out a few minutes later, it was gone.

* * *

Marsha sat in an armchair beside the window. Jules lay sleeping on the floor in front of her, his hands behind his head. Recently, she'd gone in to check on him in the middle of the night and found him in that same position. Just looking at him made her neck hurt. The drapes were open, and sunshine fell in wide stripes across his legs and chest but his face was left in shadows. She thought she should get up and do something, but she went on watching Jules's face, studying the perfect half-circle of his closed lids and the fringe of dark lashes. She was particularly taken with the way his lips pursed when he slept, as though he were eternally kissing or waiting to be kissed. Marsha tried to remember whether Craig had ever looked that way. She couldn't remember. One night a few weeks ago she'd pulled Jules into the bathroom and lifted him onto the counter under the brightest light in the house so she could study his hands and feet. He cried, but she couldn't stop. Were they like Craig's or were they like hers? In the morning, she'd tried to apologize, but Jules pretended not to understand.

She thought of Craig's phone call last week. He'd told her he was leaving town on business — Seattle? San Francisco? San Diego? — she couldn't remember, and that when he returned they would talk. Marsha had asked about the car, whether she could have it while he was away, but he'd pulled the same trick — pretended not to understand. "The car's a separate issue," he'd said, then "Gotta go, Marsha." Gotta go. They'd only been living in Dallas a week when he'd moved out. That was two months ago, but his absence still hadn't sunk in. She told Jules he was away at work, and sometimes she believed it herself. Pretending ran in the family.

She was about to doze off herself when she heard the truck with the bad muffler pull up in front of her door. The man who drove it lived directly above her; she'd seen him going out or coming home, always wearing worn-out Levis and dusty cowboy boots. He was handsome in a rough way, and it occurred to Marsha that he might help out in an emergency, if Jules was sick or something and Craig was out of town. As far as she could tell, this guy lived alone, except for a skinny black and white cat that roamed around outdoors most of the time. She'd heard him upstairs on weekends, whooping and hollering and bouncing up and down on the bed, but she didn't hold that against him. It was a good sign, she thought, that a single man would take care of a cat, and there was also something about the way he sat in the cab of his truck when he drove up, listening to the end of a song and even singing along loud enough for the whole parking lot to hear. Marsha reasoned that any man who still wanted to sing when he looked tired enough to fall asleep at the wheel would probably be good in emergencies.

He was sitting out there now. She could see him through the windshield, his hands beating out a rhythm on the steering wheel, his head back and his eyes closed. Marsha grabbed some change from her purse and went outside. She liked his voice, which was hoarse and full of feeling, but she didn't recognize the song, something about going "home to the Armadillo." He was lost in the music, unaware of the parking lot and the buildings around him, unaware even of her standing there watching. Nothing mattered but the song. Suddenly, Marsha felt like crying, and she walked quickly across the parking lot to the Coke machine in the laundry room. Passing the truck, she gave the man the longest look she dared. His hair was dark and curly, like a poodle's or a baby doll's, but the skin on his cheeks was red and pocked. He had a handsome beard, heavy and very black. Marsha liked beards. Once, she'd asked Craig to grow one, but the hair hadn't grown in evenly. The man's hands, still pounding the steering wheel, were red and sore looking.

When she came back by, he was getting out. "Hello," Marsha said, clutching the cold can.

"Hi." He slammed the door, gave it a pat, then turned to her with a grin. "It's a good old truck."

"A little loud," Marsha said.

"Yes, loud. You live right here, don't you?" He pointed to her door. "I guess you hear me every time I pull in."

"Yes, but it doesn't matter. I'm not complaining."

He shrugged, as though he wouldn't have cared if she had been. "Didn't I see you and your little boy petting Miss Kitty the other day?"

"The black and white cat?" Marsha asked, though she knew.

"Yeah, she's the only one around here, I think. The name's Wiley." He held out a hand briefly, then looked at it and withdrew it. "Sorry, I'm dirty so much of the time I just forget about it."

Marsha nodded. Wiley leaned against the truck, right at home, cars pulling in all around them.

"You look tired," Marsha said, thinking he always looked that way.

"Yeah, I guess so. I just stopped by my mom's house on the way home. She told me I looked like hell. It's bad when even your momma won't lie to you."

Marsha was about to compliment him on his singing when Miss Kitty made a leap from the second story banister onto the hood of the truck. Her claws screeched across the paint, and Marsha shuddered. Wiley only laughed.

"Sometimes I think she's got a suicidal streak," he said, scooping up Miss Kitty and turning back to Marsha. "But I know she's jealous."

"No offense," Marsha said, "but I thought you couldn't have pets in these buildings."

He looked a little hurt. "Miss Kitty's not what you call a pet." He stroked the cat and kissed her on the top of her head before dropping her lightly to the ground. Instead of leaving, Miss Kitty twisted around and between his legs, rubbing herself against his worn boots and purring loudly.

Marsha stepped up onto the curb. "Nice to meet you, Wiley. We've been living here for two months now, but I don't know a soul. Haven't even unpacked the boxes, if you want to know the truth. I keep hoping I'm going to wake up and find out it's all a mistake."

Wiley made a face and cocked his head to one side while Marsha backed toward the door.

"Must not be stuff you use very much," he finally said. "You should see my place. Whole rooms completely empty. Might as well live in a closet." The cat had turned belly up on the sidewalk in front of him, her paws in the air.

"My little boy's gonna wake up any minute. I better go in. Umm, see you later."

She opened her door, but he went on leaning against the truck.

"Hey," he said as she went inside. "You didn't tell me your name."

"It's Marsha," she replied before closing the door.

Jules was still asleep. The sun shone on his face now, and as Marsha stood over him, she felt that clutching in her throat — an excess of love that rose and nearly choked her from time to time. No one ever warned her that it was possible to love too much, but she'd found it out with Jules. Once, her voice hoarse, tears in her eyes, she'd mentioned it to Craig.

"Whoever heard of such a thing?" he'd laughed. "It's loving too little that's the problem."

But that had been his problem.

Her talk with Wiley left her giddy and pleased with herself. Turning on the radio, she danced across the living room, around Jules, down the hall and back again. She felt like going somewhere or doing something, but Dallas was a strange city, and she was a woman with a child and no car. Instead, she decided to cook. The cabinets were nearly empty, but she could make corn bread muffins — from a mix—and tuna casserole. She preheated the oven and mixed the batter before she realized the muffin tin was packed away in a box, and she had no idea which one. The move had been so hurried that Marsha had simply tossed things into boxes and taped the lids. Like the forgotten blocks of some enormous child, they were stacked all around the apartment. She was trying to decide which box to try first when the phone rang.

She chatted with her mother for a minute or so before realizing she hadn't expected to hear Craig on the other end. Was it the first time? She thought so. As usual, her mother asked about the weather. Ohio was so far away. It might be snowing in Columbus and hot enough to sweat in Dallas. Her mother could never get over how warm it was in Texas. "How do you stand it?" she'd ask, to which Marsha would reply, "I'm getting used to it." Actually, Marsha thought she'd never get used to such extremes. No matter what happened between Craig and her, she'd never forgive him for moving them to Dallas and then leaving them.

Her mother asked about Jules and about Marsha's job, and Marsha told her fine, all fine.

"Well, so how does Jules like school?"

"Oh, you know, it's going to take a little getting used to. I was afraid of going to school at first, wasn't I?"

Jules stood in the doorway rubbing his eyes and watching her.

"Not that I remember." Her mother's tone was leisurely, as though they had all evening to explore the subject. "Why?"

"No reason, really. He's doing just fine."

"Well, Marsha, if you don't have anything interesting to say, let me talk to Jules or Craig. All I get from you is fine, fine."

"Oh, Momma." Marsha raised a finger to her lips and looked meaningfully at Jules. He stomped one foot, glared at her, and then went across the hall to his room. "Anyway, you're stuck with me. Jules was worn out from school, and he's taking a little nap. Craig's still at work."

"That man does nothing but work and move you and Jules all over the country."

"It's not that bad." For a moment, Marsha was tempted to tell the truth, but wouldn't she be forced to do something, then? She wasn't prepared to do anything yet. "He doesn't have a choice," she explained. "Don't you think he'd be here if he could be? No one *likes* to work all the time."

"Not true, Marsha. Don't you read? Haven't you ever heard of workaholics?"

"Momma, Craig is not a workaholic," Marsha said, though she'd called him exactly that the last time they'd talked. "He'll be home any minute, and I don't even have dinner started."

After Marsha hung up, she went back into the kitchen and stared into the sink. It was white, so white she had to stop looking after a while.

* * *

"Where's our car, Momma?"

They were on their way down the hill again, Jules trailing a few feet behind Marsha. As they walked along, Marsha kept watch on a bank of gathering clouds. Though she'd remembered to put Jules in his new yellow slicker — it was so big his hands were lost somewhere inside the sleeves — she'd forgotten her umbrella. That always seemed to be the way.

"I've told you before, Daddy has it," she finally replied. "He needed it to drive to San Diego." Of course, Craig had flown, but it was an easy answer, one that might not raise other more difficult questions. It rankled her to think of the car sitting in a lot across town and her with a key in the bottom of her purse. If she'd any guts she'd have gone to pick it up, and if Craig had been thoughtful, he'd have dropped it off for her to use. She loved him less every day. Jules lagged behind, and she stopped to let him catch up, not scolding or nagging, though she was worried about missing the bus, not the school bus or the one she normally took to work. Today they were going to catch a city bus that went within a block of Jules's school.

"When's Daddy coming back?" Jules asked.

"Soon, honey, soon," she said. "Now, we have to hurry. If we miss that bus, we're out of luck." Marsha was also afraid of losing her job.

Several other women waited at the stop. They huddled around Jules and asked the questions strangers ask of children: How old are you? What's your name? Jules shrugged, nodded, shook his head, but refused to say a word. They smiled indulgently at him, their freshly painted mouths like morning flowers. Marsha fingered the coins in her pocket and stared off down the street for the bus. When someone yelled from across the street, it didn't occur to her to look.

"Momma," Jules said, yanking on her purse. "It's that man with the cat."

"Oh," she said, "oh." Cars swished by on either side. From between them, Marsha could see Wiley waving from his red truck. One car, then two and three stacked up behind him. Marsha tried to wave him on.

"It's okay," she called, her voice squeaky and silly sounding. "The bus will be here any minute."

"Come on, come on," he yelled, looking up and down the street. "The coast is clear, but it won't be for long."

Marsha grabbed Jules by the hand and hurried with him across the four-lane road.

"Are you sure?" she asked as she lifted Jules onto the seat and scooted in beside him.

"No, I changed my mind. Get back out," Wiley said, then laughed and glanced into the rear-view mirror. Somewhere back, a car honked, and after shifting gears noisily, Wiley pulled away.

"Where to, Madam?" he asked when they stopped at a light. His hair was still wet and it curled in uneven ringlets, slightly angelic looking and at odds with the acne scars on his cheeks and his blood-shot eyes.

Marsha looked down at Jules, who was studying Wiley.

"Gimme five," Wiley said suddenly, and when Jules complied and slapped Wiley's outstretched palm, Marsha was openly surprised.

"I didn't know you knew how to do that," she said.

Turning to her, Jules held up a hand and wiggled the fingers. "It means five fingers, Mom," he said, grinning first at her and then at Wiley.

"Where'd you learn that?" she asked.

Framed by the yellow hood, his face looked small and thin. She wanted to pull him close because in a few minutes she would have to let him go.

"I don't know." He shrugged and held out a hand. "Gimme five, Mom."

She slapped his hand and felt the resistance against her own. He shook off the hood and looked suddenly older. Sighing, she turned to the window.

"Where are we going?" Wiley asked again as they pulled away.

"Winnetka Elementary – take a left down there at the light." She pointed.

"Sure, I know where it is."

Naturally, he was puzzled as to why they would take a city bus to school, but Marsha didn't want to explain in front of Jules.

Her eye drawn to the side mirror, she saw a Triumph coming up from behind them. It was exactly like the one Craig used to drive, and for a few seconds, Marsha indulged a fantasy. Wouldn't it be wonderful if Craig pulled up and spotted Marsha and Jules in the truck with a good-looking stranger? Marsha felt happier just thinking about it, and she was smiling when they stopped at the light. The yellow Triumph edged up next to them, idling noisily. A frizzy-haired blonde was driving, her eyes on the light. The instant it changed, her car darted out into the intersection and roared away.

"Must be in an awfully big hurry," Marsha said, her insides sinking a little.

"Yeah," Wiley drawled, "Ya gotta watch out this time of day. Lot of 'em rather risk a wreck than be late to work."

Marsha laughed in spite of herself. She hoped Jules would get out and go in without a big scene. How embarrassing if Wiley were to see a repeat of yesterday.

"Not that I mind giving you a ride, you understand," Wiley said as they pulled up in front of the school. "But for future reference, a bus comes by every morning and picks up kids at the bottom of the hill."

"Yes, we know," Marsha said.

"Oh." Wiley looked down at Jules, who gazed blankly through the glass.

Marsha got out of the truck and reached for him, but he pushed her hand away without turning his head. She knew he was concentrating, trying not to cry.

"Hey, buddy," Wiley said suddenly, opening his own door and getting out. "Is this your first day?"

Jules gave a slight nod.

"Well, hell, why didn't you say so? I've never had the privilege of taking a boy to school on his first day." He shook his head. "It's a pleasure, a real pleasure."

Marsha and Wiley stood at either door with Jules between them on the seat. They didn't look at each other, only at Jules as he slowly turned to face Wiley. Wiley spoke again, his voice low and sweet sounding. Marsha wondered if he used the same consoling tone with his cat.

"Would you mind if I walked inside with you? Maybe you could even show me your room. I was pretty fond of school — once I got used to it, of course — and if you'd take me in for a minute or two, I'd owe you one."

Wiley reached for Jules's hand. "Would you do that for me, now?"

"I guess so," Jules said, scooting toward the driver's seat and letting Wiley help him down. Marsha took a deep breath.

"Thanks, Bud," Wiley said.

Jules ignored Marsha, who came around the corner of the truck and stepped up on the sidewalk. Wiley took Jules's hand and motioned for her to follow. Seen from behind, with the yellow raincoat falling past his knees, Jules might have been anyone's child. Climbing the steps and passing into the wide hallway, Marsha wondered whether passing strangers might mistake Wiley for Jules's father. Then, she saw the way they swung their linked hands, and realized this was exactly what both of them intended.

* * *

On Friday, Jules caught the bus with the other children. Marsha waited at the top of the hill until he got on then walked back across the parking lot and had a cup of coffee until it was time to catch her own bus. She was rinsing her cup when she heard Wiley on the stairs. She managed to hurry out in time to meet him on the landing. He had a shirt in one hand and a carrot in the other.

"Carrots for breakfast?" she asked. She was going to lock the door, but she'd forgotten the keys inside.

He stopped on the bottom step and smiled at her. "That's all there was. I try not to be choosy." He moved over to the truck and tossed his shirt through the open window.

"Wiley," Marsha said. "I watched Jules get on the bus just now, and I have you to thank for it. I can't tell you how much I appreciate your help and the kind way you treated Jules." She looked away, afraid she might cry.

Wiley raised a hand. "No need to thank me. I got a kick out of it. I haven't been doing so many other things right lately . . . "

"I was worried about losing my job. Jules doesn't understand that I have to work now."

"Need a ride?" Wiley asked.

"No, no, really," she said, glancing at the sky.

"Aw, come on," Wiley pressed.

"Just let me get my umbrella," she said and darted inside for her keys.

*　*　*

Once Jules went off to sleep, Marsha drifted into the kitchen for something to eat. Lately, she was starving all the time. After a candy bar on the way home, she ate green beans out of a can with her fingers. Then, for dinner, she and Jules had split a pizza. He had waited at the window for the delivery, and as soon as the boy pulled up in his truck, Jules had jumped up and down and yelled for her to come quick. She'd let Jules pay the boy, and the rest of the evening was touched by the excitement of the pizza delivery. Now Marsha felt empty again, but so was the refrigerator. She tried spreading cold butter on saltine crackers. They crumbled all over the counter, and she was picking up the pieces and popping them into her mouth when she heard a loud scuffing sound above her head. Expectant, she looked up, but the ceiling was blank, the noise over.

About the time Marsha finished the crumbs and wiped the counter the thudding began again, louder this time; then a woman screamed and a door slammed. In a moment it was all over, the apartment silent. Hurriedly, Marsha put on her robe and went to the front door. She opened it and edged out into the parking lot until she could see Wiley's front door and kitchen window. She saw nothing unusual, but the breeze was soothing and she was reminded of long walks she used to take as a child. Something about the damp asphalt was familiar, too, and bending down, Marsha pressed her palms against it. The gesture reassured her, and she went on kneeling, surrounded by the shadowy forms of cars. Not until headlights passed over her face did she get up and return to her apartment. Inside, she noticed her fingers and toes were streaked with black, and she washing them when someone knocked on the front door.

It was Wiley. "Look, I know it's late and all," he said, a little breathless, "but you're the only woman I could think to ask. I need some help here. I've been trying, mind you, but I'm not getting anywhere." He didn't say that she owed him a favor, but it was there between them anyway.

"I don't understand," Marsha said.

"Well, of course you don't. Neither do I." He paused and looked around. "Hey, I didn't wake you, did I? The light was on, so I figured you must be up . . . but, ya know, some women do sleep with the lights on." He paused and waved his hands as though to ward off blows. "No offense. Well, hell, I seem to be getting in deeper and deeper."

"Why don't you tell me the problem."

"Sure, okay," he said. Marsha sat down on the arm of a chair. Suddenly, she felt tired and wanted to go to bed.

"Look, I'll be honest with you," Wiley began again. He stopped and smiled. "I'll try to be brief, too. I've been drinking a little, not a lot, just a little, but it always confuses me. See there's this woman upstairs and she's been drinking, too. You know, Saturday night."

He looked at Marsha. She nodded and tried to look understanding. Actually, she couldn't remember the last time she'd had a drink on Saturday night or any other night for that matter. Wiley searched her face for a moment then went on.

"So, anyway, she needs someone to talk to."

Marsha waited for him to say something more, but he seemed to be finished.

"She's got you," she said. "Why don't you talk to her?"

"I tried," Wiley said. "Believe me. But I really think she needs a woman, Marsha."

It was the first time he'd used her name, and it swayed her.

As they climbed the stairs, Marsha lifted her robe and took each step slowly. She was worried about falling.

"You all right?" Wiley asked when they reached the landing.

"Yes." Marsha looked out across the parking lot. Down the hill she could see the misty aura of street lamps and the beams of an occasional car. "Don't you think you should tell me what's really going on before we go barging in?" she asked.

"But that's just it." Wiley's voice was quiet and very close. She didn't turn, but she could feel his breath on her face. "I don't know."

"Well, is this woman a complete stranger? Surely you have some idea."

"Her name's Rachel. I've known her a couple of months, but it's nothing serious." He paused for a moment and looked closely at her. She pretended not to notice.

"She's just a kid, really," Wiley continued. "Works as a waitress in a couple of different places. Seems like she's all uptight about what to do with her life, as though she had every choice in the world. I feel sorry for her, really. Think of all the letdowns she has ahead of her."

He assumed Marsha knew about the letdowns, and she wasn't sure whether to be flattered or insulted. "What happened to upset her?" she asked.

Wiley shook his head. "That's the goofy part. I have no idea. She was asking me all these questions, mostly stuff about my childhood. I answered them for a while, but I couldn't help wondering why in hell she wanted to know all that stuff. Who cares what my favorite holiday was when I was a kid?"

Marsha saw lights going off in a building down the hill. Was a movie over or what? Why would several different people, likely all strangers, turn off their lights and lie down at the same time? Would she, too, have been sighing and pulling down the sheets if Wiley hadn't come to the door? She felt suddenly grateful.

"Is that all?" she asked.

"You want more? Well, she started crying when I told her to quit asking me about when I was a kid. Then she ran and locked herself

in the bathroom. And she won't come out. She won't answer me."
He hesitated. "You know, I forgot to ask you if I could use yours,
your bathroom I mean."

Marsha handed him the key. "Don't forget to lock the door when
you leave, and be quiet. Jules is asleep."

His door was wide open, but she could see no point in his locking it. A black and white TV played to an empty living room. She
stood in front of it for a moment, watching a couple she didn't
recognize kiss and wave goodbye. The dining room was empty, too.
A cheap-looking chandelier that should have hung over a table cast
a dark shadow on the carpet. Going back to the bedroom, Marsha
flipped on the light just long enough to look around. She didn't want
Wiley to come back up and find her nosing around. Nothing in the
bedroom either except a mattress, some wadded sheets, and in one
corner an inflatable dinosaur, the kind they sell at service stations.

She'd almost forgotten about the girl in the bathroom. Part of
her wondered if there was a girl or if this was just Wiley's way of
getting her up to his apartment. Marsha was deciding whether she
should be angry or amused when she heard a small voice coming
from the bathroom.

"Wiley, you out there?"

"Rachel?" Marsha asked.

"Yeah, who are you?" the voice came back.

"I'm Marsha."

"I don't know any Marsha."

"I live downstairs. Wiley was worried about you, and he asked
me to come up and talk to you." It sounded silly. Marsha doubted
she'd believe it if she were the girl.

"What sort of sense does that make?" Rachel asked. She had a
husky-whiny voice, and Marsha tried to imagine what she might look
like. Skinny maybe, with long dark hair? "Why doesn't he try talking to me himself?" she asked.

"He says he tried."

"Oh, really?" Rachel said. "He asked me to come out a couple
of times. He told me he had to pee. You call that trying?"

"So why didn't you come out?" Marsha asked. She was staring
at the strip of light coming from beneath the door.

"Because I want him to talk to me, and if I come out, he won't have to. Where is he, anyway?"

"I guess he's still down in my bathroom. He wasn't lying to you — he really did have to go." She couldn't bring herself to say the word "pee" to someone she'd never seen. Craig had always called her a prude. He would have laughed at her now. She could almost see him in the dark hallway, those hairy arms crossed, that mocking look on his face.

"Are you still there?" Rachel asked. She sounded edgy. Wiley should have been back by now. It occurred to Marsha that her bathroom was directly below his. Imagining Rachel and Wiley in their respective cubicles made her smile.

"Yes, I'm here, and I'll stay as long as you like, but really it would be easier if you'd come out here and talk."

"Easier for you and me, maybe, but not for Wiley. The more I look at him, the quieter he gets. When we first met, it was no problem. We just went to bed. That was all there was to it. But don't you think we should be getting past that by now? Don't you think we should be getting to the part where we talk to each other?" Her words were muffled, as though she were holding a towel over her face.

"Are you crying?" Marsha asked.

"Not now. I was, but I'm over it now."

Marsha looked toward the door for Wiley. She had left it open, thinking he'd be right back. A breeze drifted through the living room and into the stuffy hallway. "Listen, Rachel," she said. "It's a really nice out. How about we take a walk?"

"It's pointless," Rachel said with a wavering laugh. "Nothing's going to come of it anyway. I'm just giving myself grief. It's not even Wiley, really. He just reminds me of somebody else. What did you say your name was?"

"Marsha."

"Yeah, that's right. Marsha, if you don't mind my asking, how old are you?"

"Twenty-eight."

"I'm just nineteen, but I'm beginning to feel like the best part is already over, like from here on out it's just living day to day. So is it?" Rachel sounded lost, and Marsha wanted to bang on the door, to kick it hard.

"You don't want to hear what I think. That would be enough to keep you in the bathroom forever. Right now, I've got my own bad times."

Marsha noticed Wiley standing in the outside doorway, an arc of hazy light outlining his tight curls. She tried to wave him away, but she didn't think he could see her.

"I want to love somebody," Rachel confessed. "But I don't want to keep giving, and giving, and giving and never getting anything back." She pounded on the door for emphasis.

"I know what you're saying," Marsha answered quietly. Her fists were clenched, and she would have banged too if Wiley hadn't been standing there.

"Nothing comes back. Do you hear me, Marsha?"

"Yes, I hear you."

Wiley moved up beside her. "Go away," she whispered, then added, "What took you so long?"

"I was reading your little boy a story."

"He woke up?" Her voice rose. "Is he all right?"

"He's fine. He asked me where you were, and I told him, and he asked me to read him a story. So I did. He fell asleep when I was half-way through, which was kind of disappointing because I wanted to finish the book. So I just pretended he was awake, and kept on reading."

"Marsha, are you there?" Rachel called out.

"Yes, yes, I'm right here," she said before whispering to Wiley, "so he's okay then?"

He nodded and gestured toward the door. "How's she?" he asked.

"Well, she's not suicidal, if that's what you're worried about. She just wants your attention — she wants to feel like you care about her."

"Wiley, is that you, Wiley?" Rachel's voice was suddenly much louder.

"Yeah, it's me, honey," he said.

"So do you?" Marsha asked.

"Do I what?"

"Care for her?"

He thought for a moment. "Sure I do, but I'm not in love with her. That's what she wants — somebody in love with her." He kept his voice low and his face close.

Marsha nodded. "Just talk to her. Tell her what she wants to know about you. Be glad somebody's interested."

Before he could say anything else, she turned and left. Outside, she gripped the wrought-iron banister and tried not to be happy that Wiley didn't love Rachel. Looking down the dark hill, Marsha searched out the building and waited for a light to go out. She picked out one window and willed it to go dark. For a moment, she thought she could do it, but the light went right on glowing.

On her way down the stairs, she tripped over Miss Kitty, who was on her way up. The cat's screech echoed across the parking lot. "I'm sorry, I'm sorry," Marsha whispered as she felt around on the steps for the shadowy cat.

Her own apartment felt peaceful, and after Wiley's place, almost homey. Even the stacks of boxes were evidence of lives being lived. Going down the hallway, she peeked into Jules's room, expecting the comfort of his sleeping face. Instead, she found him awake, sitting on the floor with a freeway of blocks around him. "Get back into bed," Marsha said, her voice sharper than she wanted it to be.

Jules flung himself on the mattress and held the pillow over his head. Marsha bent over him, rubbing his back, soothing him to sleep. Afterward, she felt hungry again and drifted back into the kitchen. A silverfish scurried into the sink as she turned on the light.

"Got you this time," she said and clapped a glass down over it.

But when she came in the next morning, somehow, it was gone.

Familiar Faces

Before speaking, Colleen takes a sip of water from the glass the waiter has just put down. "Today in the teachers' lounge we were talking about the two new restaurants in town, and I said it was just as though God had looked down and seen our plight. Just as though he'd made a commandment: 'let there be Mexican food in Ruston, Louisiana.'" She has tried to imitate the deep voice of God for effect, something she wishes she'd done for the ladies in the teachers' lounge, but even so, her husband Steven doesn't smile. Smiling herself, she goes on. "I expected everyone to laugh, but they all sat there so serious, like I wasn't joking." Steven is serious every minute of the live-long day, and she begins to wish she hadn't started this story. "You don't suppose people in this town actually pray for more restaurants, do you?" she asks. "No wonder we've been eating in the same places for twelve years." Pleased with herself, Colleen takes another sip of water and looks expectantly at Steven.

Lately, she's been working on her skills as a conversationalist, and some of the things she says could well be lines from a play, the only problem being that she hasn't found anyone who will bother to return them, not even Steven, who certainly could if he cared to. His blue eyes are fixed on the Mexican rug hanging on the wall beside their table. Someone drunk or in a hurry slung a dozen of them across the expanse of one wall. Just as she is about to remark on the slip-shod decoration, he clears his throat.

"Well, El Chico doesn't qualify as a miracle," he says, "but at least it's something different."

Colleen nods. Thinking about how little Ruston has changed in all the years they've lived here brings on the claustrophobia she developed as a child when her brothers locked her in the bathroom hamper. In the twelve years since she moved to Ruston the landscape around her has remained almost unchanged, so that she has often ached to see something erected, anything torn down. While the two restaurants were being built, she managed to drive by the sites nearly every day, and in the evenings she sometimes walked past to check the progress. In this part of Louisiana, even the weather seems to stay virtually the same, the seasons melting into one another by degrees. Now, suddenly, Ruston has a new Taco Bell and a new El Chico opening in the same month. Colleen knows that it's a fluke, that it means nothing to her life except a little more choice in where she eats, but part of her wants to take it as a sign.

Steven reaches for the basket of chips, his hand hovering until he chooses the one he wants. Colleen watches as he breaks it in half, putting part in his mouth and returning the rest to the basket. She didn't expect him to respond, and now that he has, she is unsure what to say next. Although she assumes he still finds something to say to his political science classes at Louisiana Tech, at home, Steven is like a monk considering a vow of silence. Each word is spoken grudgingly, as though he is depleting a quota.

"Maybe there's hope for this town after all," she goes on, pausing a moment to see whether he intends to answer. He only reaches for the other half of the chip. "I'm going to the restroom," she says, scooting her chair back and standing, feeling her feet slip firmly into her new slings.

Walking away, she glances down at them for a little boost. They're straw, with turquoise grosgrain edging, but the thing she likes best about them is that she bought them on sale, at 50% off. Colleen loves a bargain. In fact, she doesn't buy anything that isn't on sale or second hand, partly because two teachers' salaries will only stretch so far, but mostly because she enjoys the challenge. For years, her two sons wore whatever she brought home, but recently they've begun to to complain. The children's clothes Colleen finds on sale are often the bits and pieces that other kids refused, overly plain button-down shirts or last year's fads – garish prints and T-shirts advertising already forgotten personalities. Still, she continues buying them and the boys continue wearing them because, like their father, they are only equipped to sulk, which Colleen simply ignores.

The women's room is on the other side of the restaurant, so Colleen has a chance to scan the faces at the other tables, many of them familiar. Seeing her, they smile and nod. Some beckon her over for a word or two, nothing much. Over the years she has accumulated many acquaintances but few friends. In Ruston, friends are made during childhood or else at church. Colleen was raised in West Texas, and she resists God, so meeting people requires extra effort. For years she made do with the functional relationships she had developed at work, but the children were small then, and Steven still believed in conversation. This last year she has moved out into the community, first by working backstage with a local theater group, and then by joining the Sweet Adelines, a women's barbershop group. The songs the Sweet Adelines sing are either corny or religious, and she finds it difficult to ignore the words while staying on key. Even so, Colleen looks forward to their Tuesday night rehearsals. Often, she is one of the last to leave.

The restroom is cool, clean, and as Colleen would have predicted, empty. Although the new El Chico is conveniently located on the access road to the interstate, and a large purple and yellow billboard has been erected on the outskirts of town to alert hungry travelers, Colleen has noticed that most of the patrons live in Ruston – middle and upper middle-class families who can afford to eat out and don't mind a lengthy wait for their food. Many of the women from these families won't go to a public restroom, at least not when their own is so close by. "I just cross my legs and wait 'til I get home," she has heard them say. Colleen smirks at herself in the mirror and thinks how silly it is to feel superior about not going to a public toilet.

As she approaches forty, Colleen spends less and less time in front of the mirror. What used to be a way of communing with herself has been reduced to a momentary glimpse into the glass, the sort of quick look she is used to giving waitresses or store clerks, people she barely recognizes from one minute to the next. She's begun to feel the same way about herself. She remembers standing in the bathroom in junior high, one of the crowd of girls clustered around the mirror, pursing their lips and swinging their long straight hair, all of them too absorbed in their own faces to feel self-conscious. No more. Now, she quickly checks her thick red hair, which she wears pulled back from her face, and then turns her attention to her dress, bought last weekend at a wealthy woman's garage sale. The vivid colors — royal blue, turquoise, and lavender — swirl across Colleen's compact figure, so that she stands out in relief against the brown and ochre walls of the bathroom. Turning to see herself from the rear, she smiles. The dress is obviously expensive and apparently brand new, but Colleen got it for five dollars, the castoff of one of the town's first daughters. Garage sales are these women's way of cleaning out the closet and paying penance for extravagance. The first time Colleen went to one she was so embarrassed that she kept her eyes on the cement floor and bought something entirely too small. But that was years ago; now, she has worked around to feeling almost superior. Still, she can only manage the briefest hello for these women with their thin legs, padded shoulders, and full lips, standing in their double and triple garage driveways to oversee the proceedings.

Turning, she presses her hand against the first stall. When the door doesn't give, she goes in the second and begins the careful process of peeling down her pantyhose. Now that she has long, painted nails, she often punctures her hose, setting off a run. In the last few years, since her children took up wandering the neighborhood, Colleen has begun to indulge in manicures and facials. In short, she has become someone she never expected to be. Perched on the toilet, gazing blankly at the rosy surface of the stall door, Colleen sees herself standing in front of her high school class, mouthing words she doesn't bother listening to; sees herself, lips painted bright red, singing songs she found silly even as a child; sees herself leaning against the bathroom sink, patting a green concoction on her face. She is wondering whether this moment has already come to Steven, the moment of seeing who it is you really are, when she hears someone else's breathing. Not a movement, just a huff of air. Immediately, her heart begins heaving about like a trapped animal, but she has no idea why until she looks up and sees a man's face staring down from the top of the next stall. Instead of screaming, she simply stares up at him, asking herself why it has taken so long to catch on, to notice a presence that now seems overwhelming.

He doesn't smile or leer or do any of the things that Colleen might expect. Nor does he leave immediately. For a moment, he simply gazes down at her, his eyes grave and intelligent, the sort of eyes that might find hers from across a crowded theater.

"Please excuse me," he says in a deep, cautious voice. His head remains for only a second more, then disappears like the Cheshire Cat's. She sits, listening to the echo of his words and then to the boom of his body dropping heavily to the floor. In another second he has opened the stall door and is gone.

Talking was a mistake, Colleen thinks, because his voice is distinct and memorable. The sound of his words still inside her, Colleen drops her head in her hands, closes her eyes, and listens. If he were to sing, he would probably be a baritone. She is peculiarly moved by certain male voices, and the effect of this one, the words so proper, the tone so rich and deep, is to reduce her fear to a jittering curiosity.

"Damn it all," she says, rising from the stool, jerking up her hose so that she rips a hole just above the knee. She hardly notices it, nor does she stop to repair it with the nail polish she keeps in her purse. She does pause, however, to wash her hands, and in doing so, catches her own eyes, as he must have. For a few seconds, she looks into them, wondering what he found; then she straightens up and walks quickly back to the table.

* * *

The week afterwards Colleen sleeps less at night, sitting up to reread novels she admires. Lulled by familiar words and a weariness that resembles contentment, she pushes through one book after another, leaving those she finishes in a pile beside her bed. In class, during the day, she stifles yawns and relates the plots to her students, who sit in polite silence, stifling their own yawns.

One night around midnight, just as she has finished *Pride and*

Prejudice and is dropping it on the floor, she hears Steven unlocking the kitchen door. Two or three evenings a week, he drives the backroads around Ruston. When he first took up this wandering, Colleen was suspicious, but after monitoring the gas gauge a week or so, she relaxed. Not that she ever really worried. Divorce is the one area where they are in total agreement; both experienced it as young children and are determined not to expose Samuel and Jason. When the marriages of friends collapse, Colleen and Steven light up with a passion for one another that spends itself out slowly, over weeks or even months, leaving them flushed and more certain of their union. In between divorces, they draw apart, giving each other so much space that Colleen has been tempted to write Steven letters and leave them on his pillow.

Lying in bed, her eyes heavy, she listens to Steven opening and closing doors as he goes in to kiss the children and adjust their covers. Samuel is nine now, and Jacob seven; both have begun to resist their father's kisses and hugs. Steven wants physical closeness, but the boys want someone to toss balls and admire their skills. Colleen wishes she had had at least one daughter for Steven, but for herself, she is relieved to have sons.

"Samuel was on the floor again," he says when he comes in. Samuel slides off the bed most nights after going to sleep. Sometimes they hear the thud of his body falling, sometimes not. Samuel never wakes when he falls, nor when he is lifted back into bed. At a conference last month, Samuel's teacher told Colleen that the boy falls asleep in class and that she even found him curled up against the building during recess. Colleen is still holding onto this news, trying to make some sense of it before she gives it to Steven.

"You should have been with me tonight," he tells her as she turns off the light. "I was on old 80 between Choudrant and Calhoun coming around a curve when my headlights passed over a dog and a box on the side of the road." Colleen sighs. Here, all sorts of things end up on the side of the road – animals, washing machines, garbage bags full of who-knows-what. People just open their doors and push whatever it is they don't want out, as though the whole world were their garbage can. Steven waits for Colleen to put these thoughts away so that he can continue; he has heard them so often that he has asked her to keep them to herself. "The dog was looking right at me, Colleen. Her eyes went red in the headlights."

"Did you stop?" Colleen asks, thinking that he must have or he wouldn't be wasting so many words.

"What do you think?" he asks her in the dark, as though knowing the correct answer is a test.

Colleen hates to be tested. "You drove on," she says flatly.

Steven sighs and sits up. "Come here," he says. When she doesn't move, he prods her with the back of his hand. "It'll just take a minute."

The dog and the box are waiting in the kitchen. When Steven turns on the light, a small black and white mutt looks up briefly then closes its eyes. Colleen is slow to catch on; she doesn't understand the meaning of the box until Steven leads her over and points out the four puppies huddled in the corner. Three are tiny replicas of the mother, a mottled black and white, but the fourth is a rich and furry brown. All five animals turn their eyes on Colleen. She steps back and wraps her arms around herself, flustered.

"Poor things," Colleen says, looking over at Steven, who is kneeling beside the box, his hand stroking first one puppy then another. "Are you going to let the boys see them?" She thinks it's a bad idea. They've tried pets in the past, but the boys are fickle. Their attentions roam, and Colleen comes home to find the animal waiting patiently by its empty dish while the boys watch television nearby. She doesn't mind feeding the pet, but she does mind seeing this less-than-perfect side of her sons.

"It's gonna be tough to hide five dogs," Steven says, and she realizes that he has forgotten those other animals and the homes that had to be found for them. He thinks he has discovered the perfect gift: something for the dogs, something for the boys, something for himself.

"You might manage hiding these dogs," she offers. "They haven't made a sound."

He acts as though he hasn't heard, busying himself with lifting the mother into the box and arranging the puppies against her. The dogs are so passive that he might as well be working with flowers or a bowl of fruit. She can hear his breath coming easily now and wonders if he would have been happier as a vet or as a mother. Colleen thinks it's a shame that only she and the children see this melting, giving side, the best part of Steven.

"I'm tired, aren't you?" he asks as he follows her back down the long hallway.

*   *   *

She keeps having the same thought: "I must return to the scene of the crime."

It embarrasses her to have this cliché running through her head, surfacing at intervals to interrupt her concentration. The sentence is right out of a bad mystery, and she hasn't read a mystery since Nancy Drew. Some people want to solve things, but she doesn't. Maybe it comes from living with a brooding man like Steven, but she has come to believe that solutions are rare enough, that people tend to believe in them for the same reason they believe in God — because it makes getting through each day a little easier.

Even so, as the days pass, the man grows more familiar. She is certain that she knows him. In the morning, as she makes her coffee, she feels the scratch of his deep voice and shivers. Cupping her hands around the mug, she drinks deeply and peers out the window, expecting strange cars in the drive.

As she is pulling into the parking lot at El Chico almost a week after the encounter, it occurs to Colleen that she could be deluding herself, that the man in the bathroom might be a stranger after all. Recently, she read about a woman in Kalamazoo, Michigan, who insists that Elvis is alive and that she's seen him twice now. The first time he was buying slacks at J. C. Penney's, and the second time thumping watermelons at the Thrifty Mart. Surely the woman's relatives have tried to reason with her, telling her what should be obvious, that she has only seen someone who resembles Elvis. People's minds play tricks on them; Colleen doesn't kid herself. The woman in Kalamazoo wants to see Elvis, but Colleen doesn't know what she wants.

Sitting in the parking lot, she applies a fresh coat of lipstick and presses her lips together. They feel slick and unfamiliar. She's wearing her new straw slings again, and as she is getting out of the car,

65

she swings one foot out, so that her shoe dangles provocatively. She's proud of her feet, a size 6, a ladylike size. Most of the women she knows clunk around in an 8 or even a 9. She'd die. Once, six or seven years ago, she woke in bed to find Steven kissing her feet and murmuring. Although she enjoyed the sensation of his tongue on her toes, what she most wanted was to hear what he was saying. She remembers scooting her head off the pillow, curving her spine to get closer to his voice, but she could only catch the occasional word.

* * *

Still bloated from her lunch at El Chico, Colleen isn't hungry at dinner. She picks at her expensive frozen entree, Chicken Parmesan with green beans and then takes it out to the little black and white dog. So wasteful, she thinks, remembering the way she stuffed herself at lunch. She waited for someone to take her order, then went straight to the bathroom and sat fully clothed on the toilet. She doesn't like to think of how long she sat there, doing nothing at all, but by the time she returned to her table, lunch was waiting — a huge taco salad and a glass of tea. The ice in the tea had already melted, and the lemon slice had sunk to the bottom. Still, she drank the tea, devoured both the salad and the shell it came in, which tasted stale or maybe a bit rancid. Then she carried herself carefully back to the car. On the way home she resolved to let go of this man's face. She'd told no one. Unlike the lady in Kalamazoo, she could simply forget.

Colleen watches the dog pick at the chicken, sniffing and pushing it around on the plastic plate before taking a tentative bite. The dog isn't hungry either, but she can't bear to give up the food. Amused, Colleen sits down beside her, and picking up the hard, vivid green beans, she throws them one by one into the yard, where they stand out like caterpillars in the yellowing grass. In a moment, Steven comes out, and he, too, has his plate in his hand.

"She doesn't much like the chicken, but she's determined to eat it anyway." Colleen tells him.

"For the puppies' sake," he says, emptying his dish into Colleen's then going over to peer into the box. As he does, she notices the inverted arch carved in one side and the neat way the edges have been reinforced with duct tape. The puppies sleep in a nest of finely shredded paper, so much paper that only patches of fur are visible. Beside the box is a clean dish of water. The little black and white mutt takes a drink, then goes back to the chicken. Colleen hopes they aren't offering her too much. When Steven kneels and clicks his tongue at her, she cowers and pretends concentration on the food. Steven doesn't give up; he goes on kneeling, his hand outstretched. Colleen understands the dog's distrust; Steven does too, but even so, he wants recognition, some sign of affection and appreciation.

"They look content," Colleen says. Steven smiles at her.

"A home for the puppies, a home of their own," she chants, her words a reference to a book about a bunny that Jacob loved as a toddler. "Under a rock, or a tree, or a stone," she goes on, but Steven doesn't seem to recognize it. "Don't you remember *Home for a Bunny?*" she asks, her voice too loud. He looks up at her blankly.

"No, I don't," he says. She knows better than to be surprised. One of the more disheartening things Colleen has discovered about marriage is that sharing a life does not mean sharing the same memories.

"It was Jacob's favorite book when he was two," she explains, and then they both look inside at the boys, who are sitting together at the bar, chewing freezer-burned pizza and reading comic books. Neither has shown the interest in the puppies that Steven expected.

When she gets up to go back inside, he doesn't follow. "I'll be in later," he tells her, leaning over to scoop up a ball of quivering warmth, then sitting down on the step with it. Since bringing the dogs home, he hasn't taken one of his night drives. Instead, he sits on the porch with the puppies, rubbing each one until it goes limp in his lap. Colleen is in bed by the time he comes in, and as he lays down beside her, she smells the sour-sweetness of the puppies still on his hands.

"The longer you keep them, the harder it's going to be." She hadn't planned to say this, and the words come out sounding silly, as though she is Steven's mother. It's not fair, Colleen thinks, that we are always either behaving as parents or as children. She waits for a moment to see what Steven will do, but he goes on stroking and staring off into the yard.

Just as she is opening the patio door she hears him say, "You're right." He might as well be talking to the puppy, and for a moment, she thinks that he is. She stands and looks at him — his back is hunched, his face turned away — then she goes inside to get ready for Sweet Adelines practice.

* * *

Singing at the Peach Festival has them all excited. Because the Ruston Sweet Adelines is a prospective group, not yet an official chapter, their repertoire of songs is small, their outings brief affairs. Mostly they have performed at old folks' homes and for church groups, places where no one is expecting much. The Peach Festival performance is like a coming-out party for them. They've even worked up real costumes for the occasion — red and white striped blouses, black slacks, and black tap shoes. At a dress rehearsal, a few members remarked that the costumes were a little dull and masculine looking, so, Clara, one of the group's craftiest members, took it on herself to make each of them a belt, actually a length of wide, red grosgrain ribbon encrusted with silver and black sequins. Colleen waits until she arrives at the park to thread hers through the loops in her pants.

When she walks up late one Saturday morning, the three-tiered platform is already in place, and several members are standing close by, their faces pink and moist. They're wearing much more makeup than is necessary, and as soon as Colleen joins them, they surround her, exclaiming over how the costume suits her figure, and how beautiful her hair looks. Backing off, they cock their heads to see whether or not her features will stand out. "You don't want to look washed out, do you?" one asks, and when Colleen shakes her head, they go to work. A woman named Ruth brushes blush across Colleen's cheekbones and over the bridge of her nose; someone else outlines her lips with a red as vivid as a child's crayon. Being the center of attention causes Colleen's throat to thicken. She feels like a daughter again, standing passive while they spray her hair with lacquer, straighten her belt, and tell her not to be nervous because she is the best singer among them. Truthfully, she is only excited, but she goes on and takes the deep breaths they suggest and promises to imagine the audience as a mass of naked individuals, should the need arise.

Five minutes before the singing is set to start, the concrete steps surrounding the tiny amphitheater are lined with people. Latecomers push strollers and carry lawn chairs about the small strip of park that intersects the one-block-wide downtown area. Summertime in Louisiana is a lengthy affair, and since swimming pools are scarce, and golf courses and water slides are only available to those who have the time and means to drive either east to Monroe or west to Shreveport, people in Ruston grab at whatever entertainment they can find. Colleen knows better than to be flattered by the large turnout. Still, she is flattered, and so are the rest of them, fluttering their way to a perch on the platform.

Her place is near the middle of the second tier. The platform is new and appears to have been designed for the average high school choir, not for this group of middle-aged, Southern women, most of whom have been eating a little too much every day for the past twenty years. As she is waiting to begin, Colleen suddenly wishes for Steven and the boys, wishes fervently that they might come to hear her sing. The rational part of her knows better, knows how Steven dislikes crowds, particularly the sort that assembles for Peach Festival events, a conglomeration of people with nothing better to do. Unlike Steven, Colleen understands why they're here. Each summer she's looked forward to this Peach Festival and its modest entertainments: the Boy Scout tent demonstrations; the sidewalk sale; the parade of five-year-old Peach Princesses, each one holding a lacy parasol and sitting atop the back seat of a convertible; the pet show, and its categories of cutest pet, ugliest pet, best-dressed pet, most unusual pet. One year Samuel stood in line with his glass jar of fire flies, but he lost out to a three-legged chicken.

As the leader blows into the pitch pipe and raises her arms, Colleen stiffens, sure that she will not be able to sing. Somehow, Dorothy, the woman on her left, seems to know what is needed, and grabbing Colleen's hand, she squeezes it firmly enough for the sound to leave her throat and rise into the air. For a moment they go on holding hands, both smiling brightly into the sunlit faces of the crowd.

For most of the performance Colleen is lost in the sound, thinking neither of the words she is singing nor of the people listening, but when the group begins the hand motions to accompany "He's Got the Whole World in His Hands," Colleen turns her head and is stunned to see the face, his face, the same face that stared at her over the bathroom stall, watching her now from the audience. For a week, she has expected to see this face in grocery store aisles, behind car windows at stop lights, even on television, but seeing him now, off guard, when she can do nothing, neither run nor confront him, fills her with confusion and frustration. Her voice comes out pinched, and she forgets the hand motions entirely. While the others sway from side to side, alternately clapping and raising their arms skyward, Colleen stands stock still, and eventually silent.

The man's eyes are locked with hers in stunned recognition, and by the time Colleen looks away the song is almost over. She is just raising her arms and opening her mouth to rejoin the others when Dorothy gives her a slight nudge, and then another harder one that throws Colleen off balance. Their hands raised for the finale, the women on tier two are like large red, white, and black chickens tumbling off a fence. Colleen leans first one way and then the other, finally falling forward, onto the back of a small woman in front of her. She hears the groan of the woman and then herself mumbling, "I'm sorry, I'm sorry."

Just as she has pulled herself to her feet and is waiting to climb back onto the platform, she catches sight of the man again. Unlike the rest of the audience, all of whom are paying rapt attention to the chaos on stage, he is scanning the faces in the crowd. Colleen knows that he is trying to leave. As she watches, his eyes light on a little girl sitting with a group of children several rows away. Her dark head shines in the sun, and as she looks up at him she blinks and squints, then frowns. Calling to her and gesturing, he begins making his way toward her. The child is familiar, too. Colleen thinks she might have been one of the Peach Princesses, with her long dark hair drawn up into sleek, perfectly aligned pigtails. The girl stands reluctantly and moves off toward her father.

"Colleen," a voice calls, maybe Dorothy's. But Colleen is already halfway down the concrete steps. She makes her way around lawn chairs and people splayed out across quilts who stare up at her as she passes. Colleen avoids their eyes, trying to keep her own fixed on the back of the man's head. He's in a hurry, but the little girl slows him down, and when Colleen has left the knot of people behind, she calls out to him, "Wait a minute. We need to talk." He hears her, she can tell by the stiff way he holds his head, but he goes on rushing down the sidewalk toward a parking lot. The little girl has to break into a run to keep up. In a moment, Colleen hears the voices of the Sweet Adelines drift up the hill, faltering, individual voices trying to take up where they left off. She feels guilty for leaving them.

For some reason, she assumed he'd stop, but, of course, he intends to get away if he can. Beginning to run herself, Colleen calls out once more, "Please, I just want to talk to you." The little girl twists around, puzzled and red-faced, and when her father jerks on her arm, she begins to wail. Pausing, the man bends down to scoop her up in his arms, and in doing so, he glances back at Colleen. His face is pale and stricken. All of a sudden, she's the one in the wrong, and Colleen can't figure out how it happened. She watches him lug the girl to a big silver car. Opening the driver's side, he pushes the child in then climbs in himself. When he pulls crisply out of the parking lot and speeds away, Colleen is reminded of the woman in Michigan who is haunted by Elvis. She wonders whether the woman has tried chasing after him and demanding an explanation? And if by some chance he is Elvis and she could convince him to talk, would he be able to tell her anything she didn't already know?

* * *

Steven's car is gone when she gets home, and Colleen is grateful. A little time alone is all she needs, a dark room and a cool washcloth over her face. Once in the house, though, she hears the drone of the television, which, as she gets closer, turns into gunfire and then into that sound she remembers from childhood, dozens of horses galloping over a desert. The boys are on the floor of the living room watching John Wayne.

"Where's your dad?" she asks, and then waiting, asks again. Eventually, they turn their heads in her direction.

"He took the dogs to the animal shelter," Jacob says.

"Are you sure?" Colleen asks, and when they nod, she feels a sadness swirling through her, like something has been injected in her bloodstream. "How long ago did he leave?"

Jacob, who still doesn't have a grasp on time, looks to his older brother. "Maybe half an hour," Samuel says, his eyes blinking slowly.

The animal shelter is outside of town, a make-shift affair, little more than a rusty trailer and some leaning fences. Colleen has delivered stray animals there herself several times, and because she knows the way, she drives down the country highway as fast as the turns allow. The road is narrow and lined with tall pines, and she has a feeling of being swept through a tunnel to a certain destination. She realizes that Steven must feel the same thing when he drives these roads, going nowhere, several nights a week.

She is lucky. Pulling into the gravel drive, she sees first the car and then Steven as he emerges from the trailer. His movements are so deliberate that she has the sensation of watching him in slow motion. When they first met, Colleen assumed the slow, sure way he went about his life indicated balance and stability. It wasn't until they had been married several years that she realized she had fallen in love with qualities the real Steven didn't own. Occasionally in the last few years, she has had the sense that she is seeing him for the first time. She feels that way now as she looks at him through the windshield.

When he recognizes her car, he stops and squints into the sun, then moves slowly forward, not paying attention to where he puts his feet. The weeds outside the trailer are knee high, and as he steps into them, a grasshopper leaps into the air. Colleen's eyes follow the insect as it falls to earth; then she hurries to open the car door and get out. She wants to reach Steven first.

"It's not too late," she tells him, taking his arm and turning him back to the trailer. "Let's go back and get them."

"We can't keep them all, Colleen," he reminds her, his face puzzled, his eyes a darker blue than she remembered.

"Why not?" she asks, wading through the weeds in her tap shoes, reaching for the narrow door. "People do stranger things every day."

Winter Storms

For Lynette

"Thank the Lord for the storm!" the woman cried out.

She might have been speaking to a congregation. Her words beat against the walls of the cramped elevator, calling each soul to attention. Shelley felt the baby jump in her arms and like a good mother, she shifted her weight and began to hum "Go to Sleepy Little Baby." In the last six months the melody had become second nature. Shelley hummed it to calm herself now, too.

"Thank the Lord for keeping us safe," echoed the woman's friend. Both were mammoth black women draped in mumus and gold chains. They smiled at one another and then at the small black woman and little boy pressed between them. Shelley wanted to catch the small woman's eye, but Amelia's fierce little kicks demanded attention. Any minute she would start to scream. Humming loudly, Shelley swayed from side to side, bumping shoulders with the businessmen on either side of her. They tried to move aside but couldn't. The elevator was jammed with people from the plane, all of them on their way down to the dining room for a free meal.

Shelley glimpsed the boy's shoes between the creased trouser legs of the businessmen. She'd first noticed the shoes on the plane, when she'd forced herself to look anywhere except out the window. The shoes were stiff black leather, either newly polished or brand new – the sort of shoes boys had worn when she was a kid. Now, they all wore tennis shoes, clean ones to church or birthday parties and dirty ones everywhere else.

The boy and his mother had sat across from her. The whole time the plane circled above Tulsa, Shelley kept her eye on them. Now, she felt like she knew them or like she ought to know them. While the other passengers talked and twisted in their seats — demanded more coffee, more Coke, more magazines — the mother and boy sat quietly, dark shadows against the pink and orange upholstery. Even after the plane was safely on the ground and the pilot came back to explain they wouldn't be going on to Kansas City, those two hadn't moved.

"It's a free vacation, that's what it is," said one large woman to the other. "And did you see that indoor pool? Whew, I just wish I'd known to bring my suit."

The other woman laughed, loud and jolly. "What say we stick our feet in after dinner?" she suggested.

Just then, the elevator doors slid open, and people spilled out into the gold-carpeted lobby. Off to the left a small pool glistened. Though the floor-to-ceiling windows revealed an ice storm in progress outside, the indoor pool was so warm that steam rose from the surface.

"Shoot," cried the other one. "Let's raise our skirts and wade a little."

* * *

The three women and the boy sat near the center of the room, and Shelley took a table not far away. She watched as the two friends glanced briefly at their menus then resumed talking. The small thin woman held her menu before her face as a child might hold a picture book, her foot tap, tap, tapping beneath the table.

Shelley thought she heard the woman's heels clicking, but if she put her mind to it, she could hear anything. Several times after she'd come home from the hospital with Amy, she'd lurched from the bed, heart pounding, sure the baby was screaming, only to find her fast asleep. As a child, too, she'd been bothered by things she thought she heard, voices just outside her window or on the other side of

74

a wall. Then, a few months back, those same voices had returned, like ghosts from childhood, one a low drone, the other high-pitched and urgent, a shrill winter wind. She'd awakened to the sound of them, and like a sleepwalker, she'd risen from her bed and padded down the hall. The low drone had been Rick's voice, and the shrill one, a woman's. It was late October, a windy, chilly night. For warmth, they stood just inside the front door. Briefly, Shelley stood watching them, wondering what this moment was supposed to mean. Surely it meant something – she'd been hearing those same voices since she was a little girl. Then she'd done what no self-respecting wife would ever do. She'd gone back to bed and immediately to sleep. The next morning, looking across the sheets at Rick's face, she'd thought, surely even he would not be so foolish. She loved him and if it would help, she was willing to pretend.

But on Christmas day the same winter wind had dialed Rick's mother's number in San Antonio. When Shelley answered, the voice had asked to speak to Rick. "Are you crazy?" Shelley had hissed, as though they knew each other. She'd been holding Amy, and to make her point she'd pinched the baby and held the receiver against her mouth. Afterwards, Shelley had packed their things and called the airport.

"Ready to order?" the waitress asked. She was obviously in a hurry. Even as she spoke, her attention drifted across the room. Shelley hadn't thought to look at the menu but was embarrassed to say so.

"Do you have hamburgers?" she asked.

The waitress looked peeved. "California burger, Texas burger, or Hawaii burger?"

"No Kansas burger?" Shelley quipped, but the waitress didn't have time for jokes.

"All right, a Texas burger."

"Anything for the baby?" the waitress asked.

"She's too young for table food," Shelley said, "but, I just realized I'm all out of formula."

"We don't have formula."

"No, of course not," Shelley said quickly. The waitress hesitated a moment then hurried away.

Not along afterwards the three women and the boy received their food. Immediately, the little boy began transferring the lettuce, tomatoes, and pickles to his mother's plate. Occasionally, he took a bite of chicken, but mostly he cleared spaces and built piles. His mother, on the other hand, ate methodically, her feet planted firmly on the floor. Without pausing to speak or take a drink, she emptied her plate.

When Shelley's hamburger arrived, it came with three large glasses of milk – no explanation, just three glasses. The baby squirmed and fussed while Shelley tried to get a grip on the overstuffed burger. Each time she took a bite, shredded lettuce and little rings of jalapeno rained down on Amy's bald head. "Shit, shit," Shelley murmured, flicking the food away with her finger.

She gave up on the hamburger just in time to watch the small black woman finish the last of her son's food. The other two waited quietly, their arms folded beneath their breasts. They looked bored. The little boy stood at the window. Like his mother, he was over-dressed, and so grown-up looking Shelley wouldn't have been surprised if he'd pulled out a wallet and handed the waitress a tip. Instead, he clasped his hands behind his back and stared out into the darkness. His mother seemed oblivious to everything except the few remaining fries and a piece of chocolate cake. She took bites of first one, then the other, as though she were trying to decide which she liked better. When the plates were empty, she stood and smoothed her dress. She was thin, too thin. A belt cinched tightly about her waist didn't disguise too many folds, too much cloth.

When they left the dining room, Shelley followed. But with Amy propped on one shoulder and a glass of milk in each hand, she had to walk slowly.

"Watch out, dear, your shoe's untied," called an elderly woman as Shelley minced past. Nothing to do but keep walking. Next year at this time she would recall this moment, see herself inching across the lobby, sick over having to ask a complete stranger a favor. Only next year she'd be able to put it into perspective. Next year she'd know how it turned out.

The pool was small, just an excuse really for people to put on swimsuits and ogle each other. No one was swimming, but the two friends perched on the edge, mumus hiked up, feet dangling in the water. Their shoes, obedient pets, waited beside them. Shelley wished she could like these women.

The other one, the one she needed to talk to, sat under a large green and white umbrella. In a room crisscrossed with long shadows, the umbrella looked strangely out of place. But, then, so did the woman sitting beneath it. Her little boy had wandered off somewhere, and though his mother didn't appear concerned, Shelley couldn't help looking for him. Ever since Amelia, Shelley had felt different about kids. In a way, being a mother to one had made her a mother to them all.

"You gonna adopt the whole world?" Rick had asked her just last month. She'd been worrying over a neighbor kid who went around without a coat.

"You gonna fuck the whole world?" She hadn't raised her voice or changed her expression. She hadn't even turned to see his reaction. She'd gone right on watching the little girl across the street throw snowballs in her shirt sleeves. It didn't seem fair that some children were born to lousy parents, or that others grew up to marry lousy men. Rick sighed and reached out to touch her. She'd seen the reflection of his hand in the glass, but he'd changed his mind at the last second. When he was gone, she'd pressed her fingers to the damp glass and wondered why the little girl didn't feel the cold.

Shelley put the milk on a table, arranged Amy in the middle of a lounge chair, and bent to tie her shoe. By the time she looked up, the little boy had appeared. Evidently, he'd been in the bathroom because he was still in the midst of zipping his pants. When he saw Shelley, he walked quickly around the pool.

"That's a baby girl, isn't it?" he asked. His face was warm and open.

"Yes," Shelley answered. Her voice sounded loud in the nearly empty lobby. The two women at the pool turned around and stared.

"You know how I knew?" The boy kneeled and touched Amy's foot. She squirmed and grinned. Shelley felt a surge of pride; hers was not one of those stand-offish babies who pull away and shriek all the time.

"Knew what?" Shelley asked.

"That the baby was a girl."

"How?" Shelley asked and looked over at the boy's mother. She was still staring off across the lobby.

"Because she's wearing pink. My momma says baby girls wear pink so's you can tell them from baby boys."

"Sometimes that's true." Shelley smiled. "This baby girl wears pink because it's the only color her grandmothers ever buy."

"I wear lots of colors," the boy went on, pointing out his dark green shirt and black slacks.

"Yes, you do," Shelley said. He obviously wanted so much to be noticed. His hair was the color of pecan shells, and in the darkness, it seemed to hold light. She thought of reaching out to touch it, and was about to, when the boy's mother came up from behind.

Shelley drew back, embarrassed.

"Hello," the woman said, resting a hand on her son's shoulder. Shelley saw the boy stiffen at her touch and wondered again what was between them. "You were on the plane, weren't you?" the woman asked.

"Yes." Shelley bent over to collect Amy, who twisted and squirmed in her arms, trying to get a look at the new face. The woman took no notice, not even when Amy began to fuss. Shelley stayed busy for a moment, shifting and fluffing her child, rocking and cooing. The woman waited and stared out the window. The snow still fell, but the worst of the storm was past. "You have a lovely little boy," Shelley finally said. "So friendly and open."

The woman pulled her eyes from the window. "Yes, he is," she agreed.

It was time to make her request. "Did I hear you tell the stewardess you're from Lawrence?" Shelley's voice quavered. She'd always had trouble asking for things.

"Yes, we live in Lawrence—for the moment," the woman said.

"I couldn't help overhearing. I live in Lawrence, too, and I was wondering if I could get a ride with you from Kansas City. This whole trip was sort of a last minute thing, and the lay over.... My husband's with his parents in San Antonio. Of course, I'd be willing to help with the gas." Shelley knew she was talking too fast, but she couldn't slow down.

"Well, sure. I can give you a ride, if you don't mind coming along while I do an errand. I don't think it'll take much time, but..."

"That's fine, really," Shelley interrupted, relief shivering through her.

The woman started to smile but didn't finish. Then, with her eyes still on the parking lot, she extended a hand. "I'm Ruth," she said.

* * *

Shelley called downstairs at 6 A.M. to check on breakfast. She'd been awake most of the night. The cow's milk hadn't agreed with Amelia. Over and over, she spit it up then screamed for more. Around two, Shelley thought to dilute it with water, which did the trick. Amy sucked down seven watery ounces, smiled dreamily, and went off to sleep. Frazzled, Shelley had sat in the Holiday Inn armchair, cherishing the silence and watching her daughter's eyelids flutter. Did babies dream, she wondered. Shelley had never been prone to dreams, not the daytime or the nighttime kind. Years ago, when she and Rick had married, she hadn't daydreamed about a future with him, and now she didn't try to imagine one without him. Not that she hadn't wanted him. Wasn't he all she'd ever wanted? Even wanting the baby had only been another way of wanting Rick. In fact, she still wanted him. Once, she'd read that people aren't possessions, that you can't really have another human being, but she knew it wasn't true. Some people you could have and some you couldn't. Rick was one of those you couldn't have, and she was one of those you could.

Eventually, she put Amy to bed and lay down beside her. But she didn't sleep. She kept wondering whether Rick had tried to call home and whether she should call him in San Antonio, just to let him know they were all right. What if he hadn't called? Something twisted inside her. It was an effort to lie quietly beside the baby and try to sleep.

The desk said the restaurant opened at 6:30. By then, Shelley was starving, so she wrapped Amy in a blanket and carried her, still sleeping, into the dining room. In the elevator on the way down she thought of pancakes, sausage, and coffee.

The room was brightly lit, the empty tables covered by white tablecloths. On each table, a bud vase held a single carnation. Such pristine order sent a wave of well-being through Shelley. Suddenly hopeful, she bent to smell a flower, and was thrown off balance by Amy's weight. The bud vase toppled and rolled. Water seeped across the cloth, more water than she would have thought possible. She righted the vase and turned away.

The early risers were clustered in one corner by a window, Ruth and her son Carl among them. The same irritable waitress was serving Ruth a mountain of waffles covered with whipped cream and strawberries. To Carl, she gave the sensible food — an omelette and sausage. When Shelley approached, he looked up and reached across the table to poke his mother's arm.

Ruth looked up slowly. "Come sit with us," she said and picked up her fork.

"Are you sure?" Shelley asked.

"Of course," Ruth answered and began to eat. Being careful not to wake Amy, Shelley sat down and thumbed through the menu. She tried not to stare at Ruth, who was taking one large forkful after another. Shelley half-expected her to choke or drop a load of whipped cream on her dress, but Ruth devoured the huge mound of messy, fattening food and looked ladylike, even dainty. By the time the waitress arrived to take Shelley's order, Ruth was nearly finished.

"Don't feel like you have to stay and keep me company," Shelley told her when the waitress was gone. "You probably need to get packed." Ruth was still eating, and Carl leaned around the table to get a better look at the baby. Amy opened her eyes and dazzled him with a sleepy smile.

"No, no," Ruth said, looking up. Her gaze came from a great distance. "We're all ready to go, aren't we Carl?" The boy went on making faces at Amy. His mother studied his plate for a moment.

"Are you finished, Carl?" she asked, and when he nodded, she pulled his plate over next to her own.

By the time the waitress arrived with Shelley's food, Ruth had finished Carl's. The boy offered to hold Amy, and Shelley hesitated, then handed her over. Ruth sipped her coffee and stared out the window while Shelley buttered her pancakes and tried to think of something to say. It was awkward enough to eat in silence with someone you knew, that much more awkward with a stranger. What would they talk about between Kansas City and Lawrence? It was nearly an hour's drive.

"Did you have a nice Christmas?" Shelley finally asked.

"No." Ruth sounded irritated, as though Shelley had asked something personal. Shelley turned back to her pancakes, and when when she glanced up a moment later, Ruth was still looking out the window. The light shone on her brown skin; it looked moist, like she'd been running or had just gotten out of the shower.

"Me either. Pretty rotten, really," Shelley finally said.

"Really?" Ruth turned to face her. "It's refreshing to tell the truth, isn't it? I been lying for weeks, and I guess I'm through with it." Her face was impassive. She might have been talking about gifts she'd received that she wanted to return.

Shelley glanced at Carl, who was bouncing Amy on his lap. Either he wasn't listening, or he was pretending not to. Turning back to Ruth, Shelley met the other woman's eyes: they were dark and dry and had about them a full moon kind of madness. Shelley dropped her fork, heard it clatter as it hit the plate, felt the beads of syrup splatter her blouse.

"You wanta know why it was so bad? I promised myself I wouldn't tell a soul I didn't have to. . . "

"You don't have to tell me anything, really," Shelley interrupted.

"Oh yes, I do. You're gonna be along for the ride. You're gonna be with me when I look at that shabby apartment, and you're gonna wanta know why I'd even think of moving to a place like that. . . "

"But if it's none of my business," Shelley tried again.

Ruth leaned across the table. "But it might be, you see. Someday it might be." Then she sighed and fell back into her chair. "And if the truth be known, I want to tell you. I want to tell somebody who doesn't have any business knowing, who maybe doesn't even want to hear." She looked out the window again.

For a moment, Ruth was silent. Shelley dunked her napkin into a glass of water and was dabbing at the spots on her blouse when the voice came again—rich and rumbling—the sort of voice that should have come from an immense, earthy woman, not from tiny Ruth, strung so tight you expected her to squeak.

"My husband, my boy, and me live in a duplex near Eighth and

Michigan. Maybe you've seen those new Victorian-style duplexes on the corner, real bright and cheery looking?" Shelley nodded and smiled. She'd admired them more than once, and now she wondered about rent. Would she and the baby be able to afford something so nice? Maybe if the house were sold, and the house would have to be sold, wouldn't it? She crossed her legs and squeezed them tight. Leaving Rick and taking a taxi to the airport in San Antonio had been like doing a headstand, an easy stunt meant to impress, but now that her feet were up in the air, she realized there was no graceful way back down. "We don't live in those," Ruth went on, "but just behind them in those old, rundown duplexes that litter the street for a block. Funny to think they were new once too. Old people and old houses seem like they always been old. Can't imagine them any other way. Change, change, change all around us, but we never believe in it, do we?"

Ruth wasn't looking at her, but Shelley shook her head anyway.

"This year we had the holiday all planned. Gerald—that's my husband—was gonna work through Christmas Eve to pay the bills, and then we were going down to San Antonio for a few days. Gerald's parents and mine live there, and they were gonna wait and have their holidays with us. They say it's no fun without us there, and I can understand that. Now that I got Carl I understand lots of things that didn't make sense to me before. I was pretty pleased with the way things were working out because we were gonna have our own Christmas before we had to go down and share with everybody else. You know what I mean?"

Shelley nodded. She did know.

"Seems like when you got a little happiness everybody wants a piece. Not that I begrudge them, but you know." Ruth sighed and gave Shelley a vague smile. "My husband works for a printing company in Topeka, and his hours are long and not so regular. What I mean is you can't count on him being home when he says he's gonna be. Oh, he calls and all, but call or don't call, your plans are still ruined. It's not his fault—I know that—but sometimes I can't help taking it out on him. One disappointment after another doesn't sit well with a person. And then there's Carl. I try to explain, but he doesn't understand." Ruth waved a hand at Shelley's plate. "Go on and eat, honey. This is a long story."

Spearing a bite of pancake, Shelley brought it to her mouth, chewed, and swallowed. Carl had swiveled in his chair and was holding Amy so she could see out the window. They seemed to be getting along. Shelley couldn't help thinking that Carl could use a little brother or sister. Only children grew up selfish; she knew. Hadn't she married one?

"Christmas Eve it ended up Gerald had to work all day. He'd promised to be home at noon, and I had made plans. We were going out caroling with the church in the afternoon, and I was making a big meal for when we got home. About eleven, Carl called and started in apologizing. He was sorry, but the work wasn't finished; he was sorry, but he had a deadline to meet; he was sorry, but people were countin' on him. All that sorry, sorry stuff just made me furious. Told him it wouldn't hurt to disappoint somebody 'sides me once in a while. I wanted to say that I wouldn't have no trouble finding me a new husband that'd stay put on Christmas Eve. I didn't say it, mind you, but I thought it real hard, and when you been married to someone as long as I been married to Gerald, thinking's almost the same thing as saying."

Shelley twisted the napkin around her fingers until she could feel the blood pulse.

"You aren't eating," Ruth said. "Eat your food."

Shelley dropped the napkin in her lap and took up the fork. Pressing an edge into the stack of cakes, she watched them spring back, pliant, spongy, almost alive. She took another bite.

"He said six at the latest. Told me I could count on it. He went on and on about how hungry he was, how he wasn't gonna eat a bite all day so's he'd be ready for my special dinner. He was trying to make up with me, but I was hard with him and told him I didn't care what he ate or didn't eat because the day was already ruined." She paused. "Now why did I act that way to him when I knew it wasn't his fault?" She went silent and watched her son play pat-a-cake with Amy. "Pretty baby," she said. For an instant Shelley was pleased; then she saw how far away Ruth was, her face absent and pained, like she'd just run over a small animal.

"What were you cooking?" Shelley asked.

Ruth smiled. "A little bit of everything. Let's see now. A nice little turkey, a ham with a honey mustard glaze, fresh green beans with salt pork, mashed potatoes, cabbage cooked with tomatoes and onions, dinner rolls made from scratch. I know, I know — all that food for three people is a crime, but it was my first chance to cook Christmas Eve dinner for Gerald. Always before, Gerald's mom or my mom would do the cooking, and I'd just bring along a little something to go with — a pie or a garnish plate. They never wanted me to go to any trouble, but that's what Christmas is all about, don't you think? Going to some trouble for the people you care about?"

Shelley nodded, her mouth full of pancake. Ruth wanted her to eat, and Shelley was trying to oblige.

"Well, let's see," Ruth began again. "By six it was done, and I was rushing back and forth between the kitchen and the dining room, not mad any more, just a little hassled with all the preparations. I could tell you about the table, about the centerpiece I made and the Christmas candles I bought special, but none of that matters, does it? The food doesn't matter either, but it's part of the story.

"Six fifteen I lit the candles, and Carl Jr. and me sat down at our places. He put his finger in the jello salad, and I slapped his hand, and we were off to a bad start. He was mad at me, and I was getting mad at his daddy, so we didn't talk. We looked out the window at the neighbor's Christmas lights blinking off and on. Pretty soon it was seven o'clock, and I sent Carl in to watch some holiday special he was pestering me about. I went back in the kitchen and started cooking again. Don't ask me why; some things a person just can't explain. Once I got started, though, I couldn't stop." Ruth was quiet; her eyes glowed darker. For an instant, Shelley could see it, understand it even.

"I believe I made the corn bread first, and then I only had two eggs left, so I thought I'd go ahead and use 'em in a batch of cookies. I made peanut butter. I know what you're thinking — peanut butter isn't a holiday cookie — but I had this big jar and by that time I wasn't much in a holiday mood. I had enough left to make peanut butter fudge, but no marshmallows. I don't keep marshmallows in the house because Carl and Gerald eat 'em by the handful." She paused and made a face. "It makes me sick to see them eat junk like that. I should tell you, Sheila — that's it, isn't it?"

Shelley tried to speak, but her mouth was full of pancake and dread. She nodded and resigned herself to being Sheila.

"I should tell you," Ruth went on, "that I was watching out the window the whole time. I left the kitchen curtains open so I could see his headlights coming up the street. Looking for those headlights was a big distraction. I musta left the baking powder out of the corn bread, and when I took the muffins from the oven they was flat, flat as you can imagine, and looking at 'em made me laugh. I laughed so hard Carl Jr. came in to see what was wrong. By then it was 8:30, Carl's bedtime, but I told him he could stay up till nine. Must of been some other special on because he went back to the TV, and I forgot all about him. I found a box of orange jello in the pantry and a can of pineapple, and I made a jello mold, but when it was ready to cool, I couldn't find a place for it in the refrigerator. You'd think that would have slowed me down, but not a bit. I just left it sitting on the counter and went right on. I don't remember what I made after that, but finally I was down to making pie crust. Who knows what I would have put in it — maybe the jello. I had the rolling pin out and was leaning down hard on it, keeping my eyes off the clock. I'd just gotten the dough under control when I saw lights coming slow up the street.

"By then it was eleven, maybe later, and there hadn't been any cars in a good long while. This one came on awful slow, and first I thought the roads musta iced up. Then the lights edged by the kitchen window, and I got this feeling in my gut that whoever was in that car was looking for my address. I went on into the dining room and pulled the curtain aside just enough to see. The car had stopped in front, just like I knew it would, and two men were getting out, real slow and careful. I knew it all, then, Sheila. I knew the roads were icy, and I knew who was coming up my sidewalk. I moved over to the door and waited for them, shivering like a criminal. Behind me, Carl Jr. was asleep on the carpet, all huddled up like he was cold. When the doorbell rang all I could think was I didn't want them to see my boy sleeping on the floor on Christmas Eve. But those policemen refused to tell me what they'd come for until I let 'em off the porch. They kept calling me ma'am, and I hate being called ma'am. 'Ma'am, ma'am,' they kept saying, 'we're police officers; you don't need to be scared of us.' Course they knew it was a lie and I did, too. Pretty soon they pushed their way in the door, and I just started to scream. That wasn't something I intended, Sheila, what with Carl in the next room, but that scream just wouldn't be denied. One of those policemen held my shoulders, and the other one talked, told me what I already knew, what I'd known in my heart for hours. They said they wasn't gonna leave until somebody come to stay with me, but who was there to come? Just who? I've never had anyone except Gerald in my whole life."

Ruth went silent then, and Shelley heard a heavy thud just underneath her chair. A few seconds passed before she realized it was the sound of Amy's head hitting the floor. Carl's hands were empty, and he was staring over his shoulder at his mother, his mouth and eyes huge with misery and disbelief. Shelley felt a flash of hatred for Ruth which was quickly followed by a high-pitched whining in her ears—the noise of fear. It was all she heard, all there was to hear.

The baby was on the floor by the window. Shelley had to push Carl's chair aside to get to her. Amy looked like someone else's child. Her skin had gone white, and Shelley thought of those dolls with the porcelain heads that her mother had never allowed her to touch. Shelley was about to scream herself when Amy's face flushed red, and a screeching wail ballooned from between her tiny lips.

"Oh thank God," Shelley moaned, and gathering her baby up, she rose and walked quickly out of the dining room and through the lobby. She was headed for the elevator, but before she could reach it, the gold carpet and blue walls began to swim in her vision. Afraid to keep going, she sank down on the nearest sofa, bent over the baby and crooned. In a few moments, Amy was quiet, but Shelley stayed put. She listened to the receptionist talking to a maid about sheets; she listened to phones ringing and two businessmen complaining about missing the playoffs. She listened hard, and when the lobby was quiet, when all she could hear was her child's steady breathing, she got up and crossed the thick carpet to the elevators.

* * *

"It's a lie, what she said," Carl told Shelley. They were in the Kansas City airport, sitting in chairs facing the window. Outside, cars circled the terminal. Some parked in short-term parking; others pulled beside the curb while passengers with luggage got out. Most everyone looked unhappy or irritated. Shelley wondered how she looked. Ruth had gone to get the car; she'd said not to be surprised if it took a while: The car wasn't close by, and sometimes it didn't start right away. "Don't worry," she'd added, as though Shelley were the eldest child. Carl sat beside her and Amy lay in her lap. Outside, it was cold. Shelley could feel the chill coming through the glass.

"Carl, I'm sorry," Shelley began.

"She's been telling it and telling it, but telling don't make it true," Carl said. Shelley watched the skycaps outside stamp their feet and blow on their hands. More than anything right now she wanted not to feel, but if she had to feel, she wanted it to be for herself and Amy.

"Carl, why would your momma make up such a story? Why would she tell it if it weren't true?" She kept her eyes on the skycaps while she spoke.

Carl twisted in his seat, and when he was sure his mother was nowhere around, he leaned toward Shelley and whispered, "Daddy's just run off somewhere, that's why. Maybe it's like on TV."

"What are you talking about?"

"He's coming back to get me," Carl said, staring out the window. "He still loves *me.*"

Her teeth began to chatter, and Shelley pulled the baby closer. Amy didn't have teeth yet, but by the time she was Carl's age, her baby teeth would be loosening, her incisors pushing their way up. Shelley had assumed she had at least one true ally in Amy. Now she realized it might not be so.

"Your momma loves you, Carl, and she loves your daddy, too. Why would she want to make up things to hurt you?"

"You don't know her," Carl answered stubbornly. "You don't know her at all."

"No I don't," Shelley agreed, thinking she didn't really know anyone.

"Here she comes," Carl said, pointing out a lavender Gremlin.

Ruth lurched to a stop beside the curb, jumped out, and went around to open the hatchback. She looked to be in a big hurry. Shelley got up, and, with her one free hand, began dragging Ruth's luggage out the door. Carl Jr. helped, and pretty soon their things were piled on the sidewalk beside the car. But the lock on the hatchback was either jammed or frozen. And Ruth herself seemed stuck. Over and over, she put the key in, tried to turn it, then took it out. Shelley and the baby shivered quietly. Carl stamped his feet and glared. Cold as they were, it seemed disloyal to go back in the terminal and wait for Ruth to come to her senses.

Finally, someone came along in a Cadillac who didn't want to wait. He wanted curb space, and he wanted it now. He pulled up beside Ruth and looked expectantly at her. She ignored him. For a few minutes he waited patiently; then he quickly became infuriated. He gestured through the glass, and when that didn't get her attention, he hit the horn with his fist. The blare was shockingly loud, so much worse in the bitter cold than it would have been in summertime. Amy shrieked, and when Carl saw the baby's angry face, something snapped. He, too, began to sob.

Ruth looked up, first at the children, then at the car beside her. The driver was hitting the window with his fist and gunning his engine. He seemed to think nothing of threatening women and children. Calmly, Ruth went around, opened the passenger door, and tossed one suitcase after another into the back seat. Neither Shelley nor Carl made any move to help. When she was finished, she held the door open and motioned for them to come on. Carl climbed in back and rearranged the luggage until he had a place to sit.

"Let's get out of here," Ruth said, her first words since arriving with the car. Shelley folded herself into the Gremlin and tried to smile as Ruth peeled away from the curb. Grieving people need space, she told herself. And so at first she said nothing about the way Ruth whizzed in and out of traffic. Instead, she fastened the seat belt around herself and Amy and braced her feet against the floorboard. But when Ruth pulled right in front of a semi, Shelley had to speak up.

"You seem awfully comfortable in all this traffic," she said.

Ruth smiled a little. "Am I scaring you, Sheila? I'm sorry, really. Gerald always says I drive like a bat out of hell, but if it makes you feel any better, I've never had an accident, not even a ticket. Now

Gerald, he's always poked along. . . " Her voice faded as she realized where the sentence was going. Her expression turned first puzzled then shocked, just as her son's had at the breakfast table. "I don't even know you," she said, her eyes on Shelley, "but. . . "

"Momma, look out!" Carl yelled. Ruth swerved to miss a bridge railing, and suitcases slammed against the sides of the car. Shelley felt the sharp edge of something hit the back of her head. Amy renewed her screaming; Shelley took a couple of deep breaths.

"I'm so sorry, I'm so sorry," Ruth said, stepping on the brake until the little Gremlin was creeping along. Cars bore down around them and swept past. Angry eyes glared behind dirty glass.

"Were you born here?" Shelley asked when their hearts had slowed. Amelia still cried in gusts, and in the periodic silence, Shelley heard little tortured gasps coming from the back seat.

"No, no, no," Ruth answered with a little forced laugh. "Gerald and I were raised in San Antonio. Can't you tell? People at work are always making fun of the way I talk."

"Well, I was raised in San Antonio, too." Shelley considered asking where Ruth had lived and where she'd gone to school, but then she remembered that the San Antonio of their childhoods had been strictly segregated. It was unlikely they would have friends or neighborhoods in common.

They fell silent again, even Amy, who went off to sleep in Shelley's arms. The car was warm, and by the time Ruth got off the freeway, the windows were fogged with their breath. Ruth made several turns before pulling up in front of a group of red brick apartment buildings. They were identical, each a perfect rectangle with a flat roof and a straight sidewalk that divided the lawn precisely in half.

Turning off the ignition, Ruth turned to Shelley. She was tapping her foot again, and Shelley wanted to ask her to stop.

"You might as well know the rest of it, eh Sheila?" Ruth asked. She reached across the seat and traced an imaginary halo around the top of Amy's head. "After we finished high school—Gerald and me went all through school together—he went to Topeka to work for his uncle in the printing business. That was according to his momma's plan. Soon as Gerald graduated high school, he'd start working for his uncle. She wanted to make sure her boy had a line of business to go into just as soon as he was grown up. No way was she gonna give him a chance to fool around and fall into being no account like his daddy. I guess it worked out for the best, but Gerald didn't have much say so in the matter. Me neither. I stayed in San Antonio because our parents wanted it that way. Gerald and me were miserable, though. We weren't used to being apart. One Saturday, I packed me a little bag and walked all the way to the bus station. Been in Kansas ever since.

"For a while, we lived in Topeka, but then I got a job in Kansas City, so we moved to Lawrence. Gerald said that was the only fair thing to do cause it put us halfway in between." She went silent, staring out Shelley's window at the identical row of buildings across the street. It occurred to Shelley that if Ruth moved in, she would have the same view, no matter which side of the street she lived on. "After the funeral, I decided to move on in to Kansas City. Be easier and all. If the apartment's okay, I'll start carrying things over here tomorrow. No use waiting. A woman at work lives in one of these buildings. They're old, but she says they're clean and cheap." The material in Ruth's dress puckered and unpuckered as her knee bounced. She hit the floorboard hard enough to make the car vibrate.

"You wanna come in with me, Sheila?" Ruth asked. Shelley nodded. "How 'bout you, Carl Jr.?" Ruth opened the door and got out. Shelley heard her sigh and knew she was looking at the row of apartment buildings across the street, wondering if she could learn to be happy here. Ruth's thoughts were like waves in the air, and Shelley was adrift on them. Carl, Amy, all of them bobbed and tossed and tried to keep from being pushed under.

Slowly, Shelley opened the door and slid out, first one leg, then the other, raising herself carefully, evenly, so as not to wake Amy. Carl crawled out behind her and joined his mother, who was already heading down the sidewalk. By the time Shelley slammed the car door with her foot, Ruth and Carl had disappeared inside. Starting up the sidewalk after them, she was shoved by a bitter winter wind. The cold brought tears to her eyes, and she expected Amy to wake and wail. But instead of running for cover, Shelley slowed then stopped altogether. She didn't want to go inside. The hallways would be dark, and she had no idea which way to turn. As she stood trying to decide what to do – brave the hallways or return to the car – the blinds went up on a second story window and Ruth's face appeared. She had a blank, searching look in her eyes, as though she were still watching for that pair of headlights. Then she saw Shelley and motioned for her to come up.

Inside, the apartments were better, a little dark, but roomier than most of the modern ones Shelley had seen. The walls were newly painted, and there were only a few stains on the carpets. Carl was trudging in circles around the living room. Once, when Ruth passed through, he stopped and said, "Why do we have to move, Momma?" She didn't respond, and he resumed his pacing. Shelley knew what was going on in his mind. Kansas City was a long ways away. Would his daddy be able to find him?

Ruth went out to the car for a tape measure. She marked off each room and whispered to herself, "chest of drawers here, chifforobe there." Finally, she was finished. "I'm not sure it will all fit," she told Shelley, as though the apartment were a puzzle she'd failed to solve.

"This place is roomier than most," Shelley replied and immediately felt stupid. What did she know, who'd lived in houses all her life?

"You think so?" Ruth asked. "When Gerald's grandma died a few years back we inherited all her furniture. Some of it's so big and heavy. . ." Her voice trailed away, and she shook her head. "I promised her I'd give it a good home, but I don't know now whether I can afford a place big enough to hold it all."

She was distracted by Carl, who was standing in one corner of the living room, kicking the spot where the walls met with the toe of his shoe. The two women watched him silently, and knowing he had their attention, Carl kicked harder.

"What is it, Carl?" Ruth finally asked.

He mumbled something.

"I can't hear you, son."

"I don't want to move," he cried out. "We don't know nobody here, and nobody doesn't know us. We're gonna be all by ourselves here, Momma." He finished with a flurry of kicks. Shelley flinched, her eyes on the black streaks his shoes left on fresh paint. Ruth made no move to stop him.

"I don't want to move here either, son, but I'm trying to do what's gonna be best for us."

Carl gave one last kick and shook his head. "Daddy'll be back, Momma."

The room was silent. Shelley could hear the water dripping in the kitchen and her daughter's even breathing.

"No, son," Ruth said quietly, "he won't be." She moved in close behind him and waited until he turned and grabbed her around the waist, pressing himself in tightly. Ruth folded her body around his, covering his head with her chest and murmuring softly. At first, Shelley thought Ruth was talking, but then she heard the melody, the same song she sang to Amy: "When you wake up, we'll patty-patty cake and ride a shiny little po-o-ny."

Shelley backed up quietly until she was out the door. Then she took the stairs down slowly, one at a time, and waited for them in the car.

* * *

On the way back to Lawrence, Carl went to sleep. He lay with his head on a suitcase, mouth open, arms flung out on either side. Shelley wanted to cry for him he looked so tired. Once, she saw Ruth glance in the rear-view mirror and sigh.

A few minutes more and the sun was gone; they rode silently through darkness. In the Midwest, winter days were without dusk. One instant it was light and the next completely dark. Such an abrupt shift had always left Shelley feeling disconnected and lost. She dreaded it more than the cold and snow, though she had never heard anyone else complain.

"He's right," Ruth said after a while.

"Yeah?" Shelley answered, peering across the seat. It was too dark now to see her face.

"No use jumping into things," Ruth said. "I can't live with any more regret. It's pulling so at my guts now that I'm afraid of dying. Sometimes I don't think there's any use in our trying to change. You know what I mean, Sheila? The good Lord made us the way we are, and there's not a thing in the world we can do about it."

"I don't know."

"Just think back to when you was a kid. Have you changed all that much? I know I haven't. I remember I used to give things to my friends — little dishes or Barbie doll clothes — and then be miserable all day cause I wanted 'em back. I can't stick with a thing, Sheila, no, I always got to be wondering what if, what if I'd done something different? What if I'd told Gerald to come on home, what if I'd thrown the biggest damn fit? Why didn't I stand up for what I wanted just that one time? You know why? Cause I was afraid of being miserable about it afterwards. It would have saved his life, but I didn't do it cause that's not the way the Lord made me. I'm the sort that just caves in."

"We all cave in," Shelley said.

"No, honey, we don't. I got sisters that would have told Gerald to get his ass home."

They both laughed, and Ruth flipped on the turn signal, the east Lawrence exit already. The children were both sleeping, and the car felt warm and safe. Shelley hated the thought of leaving it.

"You know I'd be glad to help you pack if you decide to move," she said as they approached her house. "Or if you need someone to watch Carl. Whatever you need, Ruth, please let me know."

"Don't let me pass your house, Sheila," Ruth said.

"It's this one," she said, pointing. The house hulked in the darkness, but at night it looked like all the others on the block. When morning came, though, anyone passing would see the empty clay pots stacked on the porch — her plants usually died — and the blistering paint, aster blue peeling off in long strips and underneath that ugly mustard brown.

"Big house," Ruth said, pulling into the drive. "Is it yours?"

"Maybe in another fifteen years," Shelley answered, but, suddenly, she remembered it never would be, that she would be moving soon, too. "You want to come in for a cup of coffee?"

Ruth shook her head. Shelley opened the car door, and when the interior light switched on, she saw Ruth's face, soft and dreamy. She was looking through the windshield at the dark house, and Shelley could see that she was imagining a life of contentment for Sheila, her baby and husband. Then, abruptly, she turned to the backseat and fished around for Shelley's bag.

"Why don't you come in for a cup of coffee?" Shelley tried again. Ruth shook her head again and nodded toward the back seat. "Better get him home."

Shelley got out, then thought better of it and stuck her head back in the car. "You'll call won't you?" she asked. "Here, let me give you my number."

"Don't be silly. You're gonna drop that baby on the sidewalk and bust her head. Get on in out of the cold, Sheila. I know how to use a phone book."

Ruth reached over, closed the door, and put the car in reverse.

The Gremlin's headlights washed over Shelley, and she closed her eyes. When she opened them again, Ruth's car was at the corner.

Dropping the bag, Shelley ran into the street. "My name is Shelley," she cried, wanting things straight between them. Startled, Amy jerked and then screamed. "It's all right," she murmured, and like a good mother, she began to sing.

Birds

They were talking about love, and, she thought that, yes, love must be at the heart of it.

"You think love means making other people happy," he said. "You want to fix things, help everyone feel better."

Carol nodded, forcing her eyes to stay connected with his. His were remarkably large — rich, dark brown eyes that called to mind imported chocolates and coffee beans. He had told her he was from Oregon, but she would have guessed South America, so exotic did he seem. Because her own eyes were brown, she rarely noticed the brown eyes of others. When her first son had been born, she'd hoped for her husband's blue eyes, but after a couple of months the baby's eyes had turned brown and solemn — exactly like her own. With her second son, she forgot to hope, which made his blue eyes all the more surprising. She never expected to get anything for free.

The therapist's eyes were another matter, one much more bewildering. When she allowed herself to look deeply into them, she had the sensation of being both someplace she'd never been and someplace she'd always been. If she didn't watch herself, she'd begin to cry. Tears didn't deter him, though; he went right on trying to hold his lock on her eyes, moving his head into uncomfortable positions to follow her gaze.

He was uncanny in his ability to detect changes in her thoughts or a sudden shift in feelings. "What was that?" he'd ask each time her mind took off in a new direction. For the first few sessions, he was better at perceiving these shifts than she was. "I don't know," she'd say, mystified by his ability to look directly inside her. Although she'd been aware of her mind veering off, she had no idea where it had gone. He was reassuring. He said she'd get better and better at following her thoughts, and so she had. After a month or so, Carol realized her eyes were giving her away. Whenever these unbidden thoughts came to her, her eyes moved, as though she'd just discovered a bird at the edge of her vision, a pair of wings about to take flight. She wondered what this meant, that the mind looked for its thoughts in the outside world.

"You've been trying to make me feel better, too," he said. It wasn't even a question. Carol folded her arms across her chest, then straightened her legs. In her bag on the floor, two chilled bottles of juice and sparkling water – one cranberry, one raspberry – slowly warmed. She had imagined offering him one, whichever he liked, but entering his office, she'd lost her nerve. He drank too much coffee. Small white styrofoam cups littered his desk. Some of them might have belonged to other clients – he usually offered coffee when she arrived – but most were probably his. She thought about saying yes next time, though she didn't like coffee, just to leave something of herself behind – a styrofoam cup stamped with the rose-colored outline of her lips. The idea was tempting, but a little pathetic. He invited her to leave her pain. She wondered if he were serious or just trying to accommodate. If pain were so easy to get rid of, wouldn't everyone be walking around smiling? He smiled seldom enough.

Yes, it was true that she was trying to take care of him, though her attempts were so subtle that most would never have noticed. He smoked cigarettes, too. His office was always full of stale smoke. The first time he'd ushered her in she had assumed he allowed his nervous clients the occasional cigarette. Immediately, she'd given him a point for tolerance. When he lighted a cigarette halfway through their first session, she had been giving him a brief synopsis of her childhood. She wondered whether something she'd been saying had troubled him because he'd suddenly patted the shirt pocket where he kept his cigarettes and, with his other hand, fumbled for the lighter. He didn't look away, and she went on talking; both of them pretended that she was still the one doing all the disclosing.

96

That evening, when she hugged her husband, he'd smelled the smoke still clinging to her hair and sweater. "Cigarette smoke," he'd said, as though he'd discovered something questionable about her.

"Yes," she'd admitted, knowing what was coming. "My therapist smokes."

"Did he ask you first?"

"No," she'd answered, relieved. Her husband would have expected her to deny the therapist's need for a cigarette in favor of her own need for clean air. Her inability to deny the needs of others was one reason she was seeing the therapist in the first place.

"That's not appropriate," he'd said, exactly as she'd known he would, and then again, "that's not appropriate."

The second time Carol saw the therapist he didn't smoke at all, but at the third and fourth meetings, he had again smoked one cigarette, and at the fifth, at least three. Carol lost count. They were discussing how important he'd become to her.

"It's difficult for you to tell me about it?" he'd asked.

"Of course," she said, her eyes casting about the room before landing on a neat arrangement of toys on his bottom book shelf: *Chutes and Ladders*, a toddler's drum, something from *Sesame Street*. Who were the toys for? The children of clients? His own children? He was still trying to hold her gaze, cocking his head so that it appeared to be resting on his shoulder. Carol wondered whether he had an understanding wife who rubbed his neck before he went to sleep at night.

"How does it feel to let me know that I'm important to you?"

"Vulnerable," she said. "Scared." She wished he wouldn't force her to spell everything out. She wanted to be honest, but in this case, she couldn't quite say everything she felt.

On the long drive home, Carol thought of him, saw his face in her mind, or at least parts of his face — his beard, his eyes, the way he rubbed his mouth with the back of one hand. He wore a silver bracelet on his left wrist, a flat band that looked as though it were there for life. The bracelet flashed in her head at odd moments, as she was driving down the highway, or at night when she turned out the lights. Carol wore a silver bracelet, too. Hers was fourteen years old, one of the few things she hadn't let go of. It slid up and down her wrist every day, reminding her of who she'd been, who she had hoped to be. She wondered if he'd noticed it.

Transference was nothing new to her. Just out of college, she'd worked three years in a psychiatric hospital with adolescents. Some of the children on her unit had developed intense attachments, hating and loving her fiercely. Not loving them back had been the hardest part of the job. "You need to figure out the difference between caring and loving," the social worker on the unit had told her. She never had.

At thirty-six, she still didn't have a clue. She'd been seeing the therapist for only a month when she began carrying him about in her head. The feelings had come on quickly, welling up and pressing against the inside of her chest, threatening to burst out and make a fool of her. Following him down the hall to his office one day, she'd been surprised by a desperate impulse to throw her arms around his waist and bury her face in his shirt. The only way she'd kept from doing it had been to fold her arms under her breasts and hold them there. You don't know this man, she kept reminding herself, but in her heart she believed she did. In the last month she'd lost five pounds. Her husband fretted and sent her sad looks across the bedroom. She felt sad, too, but it was a sadness she savored. The flip side was giddy happiness. She laughed more and danced with her baby across the living room. In the morning and evening, she stood in front of the mirror, watching her face and wondering whether he saw what she did. Wasn't it a prettier face than she'd remembered? Carol had told her therapist he was important to her, but she hadn't told him that it felt exactly like love.

The highway she drove cut straight through farmland — black fields occasionally interrupted by the small square of trees, and inside the square, a frame house, a barn, and a silo. At dusk in early winter, the world was all some shade of brown or gray, the coming darkness seeming to sink into the land, the trees, the gray asphalt of the road, everything slowly taking on shades of black until, finally, the only bright spots left were her headlights on the road. She was wondering about love, about whether it's possible to love people out there in the world or only the ones we create in our heads, when the new thought came. By now, she was used to following them. Her eyes shifted, and she gazed out across the darkening sky. The bird taking flight was Beth. Thirteen years and a thousand miles separated them, but Beth was determined, and Carol had never been any good at denying her.

* * *

The summer before her senior year at the university, Carol had taken a job at the Austin State School, an institution for the mentally retarded. The job was permanent, but Carol had only planned to work for three months or until the fall semester started. The person who read her application must have guessed as much; she placed Carol on the unit for profoundly retarded teenage girls, where turnover was so high that three months seemed a reasonable stint. Carol saw the job as a chance to be with children again. Much of her childhood had been spent taking care of her mother's other children, and though she was glad to be out from under the constant responsibility, pleased to have only herself to nurture, it didn't seem quite enough sometimes. She needed to be needed.

Before processing the paperwork, someone in personnel took her for a visit, a test of sorts. No point in wasting a lot of people's time if she were only going to back out the first day on the job. Carol knew she wouldn't, even if the room were full of snakes, but they couldn't have known that about her. Still, she wasn't quite prepared. The room was bigger than she'd imagined, and much emptier. No toys on the floor or posters on the wall, no games in progress, no music. Nothing except the mustard-colored tile walls, the off-white linoleum floors, the mingled smell of disinfectant and urine, and the children. Like strangers waiting in a terminal, they sat around the edges of the room. Propped against the walls, eyes directed toward the empty center, they dreamed their separate dreams. Some waved fingers in front of their faces, going cross-eyed as they followed the motion. Others simply sat. A few had to keep moving. They roamed the room, from corner to corner, restless, as though someone had whispered in their ears, told them it was time to go home.

Carol was a little shaken. She stood off to one side with someone from personnel, a couple of other prospective employees, and the unit supervisor. They were making small talk, something about the heat. "It's always nice and cool in here, anyway," the unit supervisor assured them. She was a small black woman who rocked back and forth on the balls of her feet, giving the impression that she had more energy than the job required. The children behind her were static as statues. Carol nodded and smiled and cast her eyes around the room, looking for something, anything, to set her at ease. For some reason, it was then that Beth, one of the roamers, edged over and pressed herself against Carol, clucking and squeaking. If Carol had closed her eyes, she would have imagined some impossibly-colored bird perched high above the ground in the rain forests of Brazil. But her eyes were open, and so instead she saw a tall thin girl, wearing shorts a size too small and nothing else. Her face was blotched and scarred, her blonde hair fuzzy and chopped-off looking, like an old doll's. Carol reached for her hand, and the girl latched on, jumping up and down in place, squealing louder and louder until the room vibrated with the sound. Whatever was left of the conversation died away.

Eventually, they all stood staring, even the unit supervisor, but at Carol, not at Beth. Carol was reminded of times when she'd taken her three sisters to the grocery store. She'd been barely sixteen, just old enough to drive; they'd been six, five, and four. Sometimes they ganged up on her at the checkout stand, crying and begging for cookies or something else she didn't have money for, making a scene so that other shoppers turned and stared. Their looks were directed at Carol. Couldn't she do something, their faces said. "Stop it, stop it," Carol would hiss at the girls, one part of her furious, the other part sad. They'd been given so little of what children need to sustain them.

"Beth is our problem child," the unit supervisor told the others, and then to Carol, "she seems to like you." Carol sensed that it was both something she meant and something she didn't mean. Beth might have liked the color of her dress, or the way she smelled, maybe even the arrangement of her features, but certainly not Carol herself. They didn't know each other, the unit supervisor's eyes said, and no matter how much time they might spend together, they never would.

Contrary to what Carol had imagined, the job was mostly physical: mopping the floors and cleaning the walls in addition to feeding, toileting, showering, dressing and undressing the girls. Between chores, the workers made half-hearted swipes at using B-Mod, popping M&Ms into open mouths when the girls sat on the toilet or thrust a hand into a waiting sleeve. No one much believed in it, not even Carol, who had studied Skinner. Keeping them clean and safe was all that was really expected and all that could reasonably be done. The biggest girl on the unit was aggressive and enjoyed terrorizing the small, passive hand-wavers. One day, when Carol wearily pulled her off a much smaller child, the girl turned and bit into Carol's shoulder as though it were a piece of meat. Blood soaked her cotton blouse, pasting it to her shoulder. Afterwards, the girl was calm and allowed herself to be showered and dressed for bed without a fight. "Maybe you should let her bite you every night," the others joked.

Even the biter steered clear of Beth, though. Everyone did, except Carol. Hurting other people was one thing, but hurting yourself was quite another. "Seems to me living in this hellhole would be punishment enough for that child," one of the day workers told Carol. "Why's she wanna go making more for herself?" Carol didn't know. She didn't try to argue with the old hands who shook their heads when they saw Beth scuttling behind Carol, but she didn't argue with her feelings, either. Sometimes we pick the people we love, she wanted to tell them, and sometimes we don't.

Pinching herself might have been Beth's way of remembering she was alive. All day every day she strolled about the room, fingernails pressed into her flesh. When the workers cut her nails shorter, sometimes trimming them down to the quick, Beth simply pressed harder, leaving red blotches, if nothing else. Her body was a mass of tiny crescent-shaped wounds, some fresh, some healing, and underneath, hundreds of pink and white scars.

When something upset her, and any little thing might, the pinching turned to slapping. Her usual grunts and squeaks became shrieks, sounds so loud and frenzied a bypasser might have imagined some enormous bird had just awakened to find itself trapped, walled in. On long, thin legs, she circled the room, first walking, then running, her speed building while she slapped her face with one hand then the other. Years of this ritual had left her cheeks calloused, the skin thick and a little yellow. If slapping didn't bring immediate relief, she'd strip. Usually, her clothes came off quickly and easily, but sometimes the need to move got in the way of undressing, and she'd take off in a blind run, a shirt still wrapped about her head and arms, her screams muffled as she collided with walls and people. No one ever got used to seeing her this way – her thin, splotched body streaking past, screeching and slapping, screeching and slapping – but interfering only made her worse.

On bad days, she beat her head against the wall, pounding away at the same spot, a spongy half-dollar-size lump precisely in the middle of her forehead. The swelling went up and down, but the lump stayed, as permanent a feature as any other. Sometimes, when the spot was angry and bruised, Carol imagined a third eye rising to the surface and Beth beating it back down again. Headbeating was a serious matter, and whenever she started in, they had to wrestle her to the ground and force a football helmet onto her head. They used shoelaces to secure it – tying them to the face guard and then around her neck and back again. Usually, the helmet did the trick. A few minutes wearing it and Beth was strutting around the room, clucking and smiling shyly.

Occasionally, nothing worked, and the doctors had to order a straitjacket and an injection to put her to sleep. Carol remembered coming to work and finding Beth sleeping, the sheet wounded tightly around her, only the top of her head or the sole of one foot protruding. Bright, beckoning light poured from the windows across rows of white beds, but Beth lay so still that Carol had to reassure herself by touching her; once, she sat down on the bed and surprised herself by gathering Beth into her arms. She sat that way for several minutes, with Beth's head cradled against her chest.

Life was calmer while Beth slept. Mealtimes, she was always starving, and after wolfing her own food, she grabbed whatever she could off the other children's trays – large pieces of meat or a whole serving of cake – jamming it into her mouth and dashing away. The duller ones never noticed; often, she stole the very piece of food they were reaching for, whisking it off the plate so quickly that their hands would hover over the empty spot, no longer sure where to land.

Given the chance, going to and from the cafeteria or when the unit door was unlocked, Beth bolted; her long thin legs carried her easily down the hall and out the front door. Beth had the grace of an athlete or a dancer, and Carol loved to watch her run. One night after supper, Beth darted from the wavering line of children and out the door. Carol took up the chase, following her through the fields and around two buildings, staying close, but being careful not to catch her. Beth screeched – her happiness noise – and waved her arms like wings. Carol intended to let her go as long as she liked, but Beth tired quickly. When Carol reached her and saw the sticky whiteness of Beth's face, she was frightened. Immediately, Carol pushed Beth down into the grass then sat beside her until she seemed herself again. It took a while. Even though Beth was seventeen and a native Texan, she had never experienced the heat and humidity of August. Her skin had never been tanned, and in those small protected spots where she didn't have either scabs or scars, it was as milky and translucent as a baby's.

By the end of August, Carol was relieved to leave the rest of it. Early on she had bragged to a friend that she could eat a tuna sandwich while she mopped up pee, but being able to and wanting to were different things. Even waitressing was less exhausting. But how could she leave Beth? For a while, it seemed she'd have to. Beth's parents, who lived a hundred miles down the highway in the direction of Dallas, had stipulated that Beth couldn't see volunteers or leave campus. As far as Carol could tell from reading the charts, Beth had never been off the school grounds, not once in fourteen years. No one knew why. Not even the parents, evidently, because when Carol phoned and asked if she could do volunteer work with Beth, they seemed only surprised and uncomfortable. It had been two years since they'd made the drive to see Beth. "Why do you want to do this?" they'd asked her. Carol couldn't remember just what she'd told them. Had she explained about her brother and sisters and the years she'd spent caring for them? If she had, she did not say what was in her heart, that in some mysterious way, Beth seemed even more her kin than they did. In the end, they were gracious enough, and when Carol hung up, she had their permission and an easy sense of her own superiority. Doing the things other people neglected was the one sure way she had of feeling good about herself.

She went twice a week, first just for walks around the building, then for walks around the campus. One day they ventured into the school's chapel to admire the stained glass windows, long panels of red and purple that turned the light inside dense and otherworldly. They sat together in a pew in the empty chapel, Carol watching Beth's upturned face, all wide smile and dazzled eyes. Beth twisted and turned; her squeals echoed across the empty room. Carol sat beside her and hummed the Methodist hymns she'd learned in childhood.

Their first trip off campus was on a sunny late-September day. In Austin, such days felt more like summer than fall. Tar still bubbled on the street, and the handles of car doors were hot to the touch. While she stood and waited for someone to come and unlock the unit door, Carol put an eye to the small window. Beth was striding naked across the room. Otherwise, she seemed calm enough, and when Carol was let in, Beth ran to her, squealing and grinning. They walked hand in hand to the clothes closet, and Beth stood by calmly while Carol rummaged through other children's clothes, trying to come up with a decent outfit. Beth's clothes came from donations stored in another building. Whenever necessary, workers were supposed to go over and sort through the stacks, but no one bothered for Beth. She so seldom wore clothes. Because the other girls were all much smaller, most of them the size of six-year olds, the pink corduroy pants Carol put on Beth looked more like pedal pushers. "Good luck," the other workers called out as they left. Carol smiled and waved, pretending luck was something she needed.

She had thought this trip through in advance. In the front seat, Beth would be a distraction, maybe even dangerous, but in the back, secured by the seat belt, she would be safe. As they putt-putted up the main road and turned right at the brick columns, Carol felt a rush of pleasure, as though she were doing something forbidden, as though they were prisoners making a reckless mid-day escape. In fact, they were two young women close enough in age to be sisters, and one was taking the other for ice cream and to the park. Stopped at a light, Carol wondered which they should do first. Beth was screaming, but then she was always making some noise, so when the light turned, Carol only glanced in the rear-view mirror and drove on.

She'd only gone a few blocks more when she felt the uncomfortable stares of strangers in other cars; everyone who passed looked in at them and then sped on. Sighing, Carol pulled to the side of the road and turned to look herself. Beth was still strapped in her seat, her legs folded neatly under her, in the manner of a Buddhist monk. She was gazing ahead, through the windshield and traffic straight to the horizon. What could she possibly be seeing? Her pupils were so dilated they resembled black planets surrounded by a thin ring of blue iris. She was completely naked and slapping her face so fiercely that her hands were a blur in the air. "Beth," Carol sighed, and then again, "Beth." Heading back, Carol realized they'd been gone all of five minutes.

The next week Carol and the nurse corralled Beth in the clothes closet, and between them, taped tongue depressors in a neat fence around the crook of each arm. While they worked, Beth clucked and squeaked, rising slowly on the balls of her feet and coming down softly, as though not to disturb them. If she wasn't distressed, Beth was like any other child. She enjoyed being touched. Carol noticed the planets in her eyes were more distant this time. Perhaps the doctors had changed her medications again. Beth was an institutional guinea pig: She took drugs to control her seizures, balance her metabolism, build up her iron reserve. Then there were the ones that were supposed to control her "self-abusive tendencies." These changed in number, color, and shape, but always, Beth's little paper cup overflowed. The pleated white cups reminded Carol of birthday party favors, something the solicitous mother would place beside each plate, along with a blower and a balloon.

When Carol and the nurse had finished, they let Beth walk away from them. With her arms stiff at her sides, Beth marched around the room, clucking softly, a small wrinkled smile on her face. Clearly, Beth liked the tongue depressors. Carol and the nurse nodded to each other, pleased with themselves, then watched as Beth came by. When restrained by the strait jacket she wore the same look – safe, almost cocky.

Over the next six months the two of them went to parks, the rose garden, Carol's home, even Armadillo World Headquarters, the beer garden and concert hall where Carol waited tables. Sometimes they just drove out in the country, and Carol let Beth run. Maybe these were their best times: Beth roamed wherever she liked; Carol followed and waited for Beth to glance back, that wild look of happiness on her face. As fall passed into winter, Carol phased out the tongue depressors. Anything heavy over her arms was enough to give Beth a sense of control, a coat or even a sweater. By spring, Beth was going out in shirtsleeves. Carol was giddy with Beth's progress. She began to dream of Beth at night, and in these dreams, Beth not only spoke, she showed Carol the world — lightning storms and the webs of spiders stretched against rocks, things Carol had seen before and things she hadn't. During their time together, Carol listened more closely, waiting for that first word. She believed it would come.

One afternoon in late spring, on their way back to the school, they passed a carnival in the parking lot of the auditorium. It was only a small traveling affair, not much more than arcades and cotton candy, but it had drawn a respectable crowd, mostly people coming home from work and in need of a lift. A ferris wheel rose in the midst of the booths — turning, turning — and music from the carousel drifted through the open car windows. "What the hell," Carol said, swerving into the parking lot. When Beth spied the lights she stamped her feet on the floorboard of the old Volkswagen, squawking and screaming, a whole pet store full of bird noises in the back seat of Carol's small car.

Hand in hand, they walked the littered avenues. Beth's excitement was like friendly electricity, traveling through her fingers and passing into Carol's. Even when she stumbled on a popcorn box and fell to her knees, Beth didn't let go. Laughing, Carol pulled her to her feet and pointed out the lights of the ferris wheel. They stood together looking up, Beth squealing softly, giving voice to Carol's happiness. Sometimes Carol wanted to make something mysterious or occult of their friendship, twin souls reunited after hundreds of years. Other times, she realized that with Beth she was able to let go and be something she'd scarcely ever been — a child.

At the carnival Beth was no different than the rest of them, jumping up and down and screaming, full of noisy pleasure. They watched while a teenager cursed his luck at the arcades, kicking the side of the booth with the toe of his heavy black boots, scowling at everyone who dared look his way. They listened to the screams of teenage girls on the Tilt-a-Whirl and the high-pitched cackle of the witch at the Haunted House. Everyone was busy letting go of feelings. If she squinted her eyes, Carol could see a vapor of emotion rising slowly into the darkening sky. Out in the parking lot, the rest of them would tuck away what was left of their feelings and climb back into their cars for the silent ride home. If they were disappointed when they got there, they might slam a few pans or a door before settling down for the evening. It was easy to forget that Beth couldn't do the same.

That night, Carol stood outside the unit, her hands on the cool brick wall, and listened to Beth howl inside. Though she had tried not to notice, Carol knew that for Beth, returning home was becoming more and more difficult. Her agitation began as soon as they parked in front of the building and increased as they walked down the hall toward the locked door. She didn't want to go in, and she would cling to Carol, moaning and squealing, until Carol had to call for help to peel her off. The other workers sighed and turned their faces away. One of the older ones spoke up: "You aren't doing her no favor you know." Until that night, Carol had ignored them. As she stood outside and listened to Beth beat her head against the wall, she could ignore it no longer. The sounds seemed to go on and on, the monotonous pounding and the loud, agonized screams. "Why don't they stop her," she said aloud, and then "please, please stop her." She sank down in the bushes, rested her head against the wall, and sobbed. In time, she realized it was quiet inside. They would have her in the office now. Someone would be holding her down, someone else calling in an order for a sedative or a straitjacket or both. Out there in the bushes, Carol thought of beating her own head, even tried it once or twice, experimental tappings; then disgusted with herself, drove home.

A few more times. She took Beth out a few more times, but only on campus, short visits that left them both dissatisfied. Beth had seen the world now, and knew what she was missing. Carol couldn't help wondering whether Beth's parents had been right in withholding it for so long. She never said goodbye; she simply stopped going. And for years afterward, she waited for the love to give up and leave her. The dreams came less and less often, but they didn't stop until she married and moved away from Austin, until she had children of her own and so much to do that she fell each night into a dark, seamless sleep. Something in her refused to forget, though. Every time she went to Austin — twice a year at least to see her husband's parents — she drove past the school, all pink bricks and white columns, and wondered where Beth was, what she was doing just then. As a child, Carol had often been forced to give up the people she loved. Oddly, instead of learning to say goodbye gracefully, she'd turned stubborn, resisting letting go at all.

* * *

She was practically home. In a few minutes, she'd crest a small hill and see the green highway sign: Iowa State University, ¼ mile. In ten minutes, she'd pull into the parking lot of the daycare center and hurry in to find her baby son. He'd be toddling around the open room, clutching a block or a spoon and muttering to himself. The therapist wouldn't be far behind. Like her, he commuted to Des Moines from a town thirty-five miles north on the interstate. Ironically, they lived only blocks apart and had sons in the same elementary school. Sometimes she saw him at school concerts or carnivals, caught his eye for an instant before both of them had to look away. All that emotion, yet in some ways they would always be strangers. Carol imagined him now, his brown eyes focused on the road ahead, his car pushing through her memories. She watched while his hand strayed from the steering wheel to his beard. "What was that?" he asked, his words loud in the quiet car. Beth's cries still echoed across the winter fields. Carol wasn't crazy. She knew she was the only one who heard them, that something perverse and childlike in her would go on hearing them for the rest of her life. Still, she trusted he'd be looking, squinting into the darkness, his head cocked for a glimpse of the rare bird she'd loosed on these Iowa skies.

Under the Bright Sky

For Debra Weiner

"There's a full moon tonight," June said. She was pushing her way out the door of the cold vault, her arms full of lemons. As usual, she carried too many, and on the way to the bar, several got away and rolled around her feet before coming to rest in out-of-the-way places. At any given time, at least one lemon rotted behind the sink or under the fryer. Always, the air was tinged with the acrid smell.

"Yeah?" Eddie said. He was swinging longnecks from a box and stacking them in the cooler. His hand moved so fast it was a blur in the air. June expected him to break one; she waited for the moment, but it never came. Disappointed, she returned to the lemons, hoisting the big cutting board onto the bar and herding the fruit over next to it. In the process, two more lemons went over the edge and plopped to the floor. June pretended not to notice. Perched on a stool, she began slicing what was left into wedges. Eddie stopped to watch her then bent to collect the runaways.

"Your dad would shit if he saw the sloppy way you do things around here," he said, getting down on all fours and reaching into a corner. "If I didn't pick up after you, we wouldn't be able to walk across the floor."

"Nobody asked you to pick up, Eddie." June held out a hand for the lemons and felt his fingers slide across hers. Touch had taken on a whole new meaning for June. In the last month, she and Eddie had begun slipping out during breaks to a spot behind the building. Eddie leaned against the building and she leaned against Eddie. June assumed her dad knew what they were up to; every day, she waited for him to take her aside. But what could he say, anyway? When he stayed out all night he never bothered with explanations. He just sauntered in on Sunday morning, carrying a newspaper and a bag of donuts. It would have been easy to pretend he'd just gotten dressed and gone out for a minute, except for the smells clinging to him. One whiff and June would back away, his signal to drop the donuts on the table and walk down the hall to the bathroom. After she heard the spray of the shower, she'd sit down to eat.

"Your dad's late," Eddie remarked. She felt his gaze slip from her eyes to her breasts to her rear end perched on the stool. Flustered, she cut faster. "Watch out!" Eddie cried. "You'll cut yourself."

"It's hot as hell in here," she complained, dipping her fingers in a glass of ice tea and rubbing them against her forehead. Drops dribbled down her eyebrows, flooding her lashes. For that instant, she was content. So many things displeased her—from the shape of her body to the fact that she had no real mother to speak of. She found it difficult to be happy for long.

Eddie went back to the beer, giving her a chance to stare at him. Again and again, her eyes returned to a configuration of freckles that sloped across the ridge of his nose then twisted back toward his right eye. She liked his freckles and the soft way he ran his hands over her, but she hated his silliness. Even at eighteen, he was more boy than man, content to fiddle his time away in this low-down bar. June knew the Split Rail was her dad's best friend, his real home, his whole life. But no way would she give herself to some other man who'd spend his days worrying about beer sales and whether or not to pave the parking lot.

"Don't forget to mop," she told Eddie when she finished the lemons.

He sighed. "Don't boss me around, June. Your dad may own this place, but you work here same as me."

"I'm trying to help you, Eddie. He'll be here any minute, and you're not even close to being done."

"Neither are you, Missy," he said and returned to the boxes of longnecks.

June rolled her eyes. He was so corny, always calling her Missy and taking her to the playground at midnight. Last night, they'd spent so much time whirling on the merry-go-round June had been forced to leap off and run into the darkness to throw up. Eddie had been very nice about that: he'd wiped her face with a handkerchief and gotten her a Coke to get rid of the bad taste. Sometimes, she thought he'd go straight from being a kid to being a grandpa.

"Okay, Eddie," she said. "Let's just both get busy."

By four o'clock, the bar was stocked, the floors were mopped, and the chairs were down. Eddie had gone home to change, and June was sitting at one of the tables in the back, eating french fries drenched in catsup. The messier her food, the better she liked it. And she liked food.

Supposedly, her mother ate like a bird. "Hardly ever saw her put a bite in her mouth," June's grandmother had remarked one day while June put away a third piece of angel food cake. Out of spite, she'd eaten a fourth. June knew her mother was fond of cats and country music, that she made a living cutting and curling other people's hair and was prone to do crazy things with her own. Out of these few details, June had fashioned a sketchy picture of someone who looked and acted like Flo on that old show about waitresses in a diner. June told herself she was better off without a mother like that.

The back door slammed, and her dad's voice called out "Sugar?" Jumping up, June dropped the plate — french fries and all — into the nearest trash can and wiped her mouth with the back of her hand. Her daddy would probably have Nick with him, and she didn't want them to catch her eating. She liked to give the impression that she, too, ate like a bird. That way no one thought to blame her for her plump rear end.

Once upon a time, Nick and her dad had been best friends. Now, Nick was practically a star, the only one in Gabe's old band who hadn't given up on music. "He's a real musician," Gabe told her. "Got his fingers on the guitar before his eyes are opened good, and he don't take 'em off 'til he passes out at night."

On the album cover Nick was serious and handsome, his eyes

staring right into hers. She liked the way he hooked his thumb into the loop of his tattered Levis. And she loved his voice, which was warm and husky but smooth, like the chocolate frosting she licked off her fingers. Her grandma always tut-tutted and told her to save the icing to eat with the cake, but you couldn't suck cake off your fingers. June expected the real Nick to be like frosting after it's on the cake, sweet but ordinary enough. She was wrong though.

He came walking in behind her dad, shoulders hunched forward a little, wearing a wrinkled black cowboy shirt and jeans, maybe the same ones as in the picture. He had on scuffed lizard cowboy boots, one pant's leg tucked into his boot and the other left out. As soon as he saw June, he grinned and whistled. He was even better than the album cover.

"Everything ready to go, sweetheart?" her daddy asked.

"Sure thing," she replied, glancing around. Suddenly, she saw the bar as Nick must see it: the cracked and stained concrete floor; all those beat-up, rusty folding chairs; neon beer signs, hanging crooked on the cinderblock walls, flashing off and on, off and on—all of it shabby and miserable looking. And in the middle of it all her dad stood there beaming, like someone had just handed him a hundred dollar bill for doing nothing at all.

"Nick, this is my daughter, June," he said, one hand on Nick's shoulder, one hand on hers.

"Lucky girl. She doesn't look a thing like you," Nick said. June knew what he was thinking, that she took after her mom, but she also knew he wouldn't say so. People avoided mentioning June's mother, even people like Nick, who surely must have known her.

"Well, she may not look much like me, but looks are only part of what you give a child." Gabe's smile had faded, and he peered at June, as though she were a stranger. She pulled away.

"Can I get you a beer?" she asked Nick. The question was second nature.

"Maybe later, thanks," he said. "I better round up the rest of the band. We gotta set up if we're gonna play tonight." He turned and began walking toward the stage door, then stopped and called over his shoulder, "Nice to meet you, June. I been looking forward to it all day."

"Yeah, me, too," June replied. When he was gone, she dropped into the nearest chair.

"Mighty proud to have someone of Nick's caliber here at the Split Rail," Gabe said. June jumped. She'd forgotten her dad. "Gonna be a big night," he went on, patting the top of his daughter's head. "You gotta beer for me, Sis?"

"Sure, Daddy." As she crossed the floor, she spun in tight circles, her arms flung out on either side. June wished she knew how to dance, really dance so that anyone watching would have to catch his breath.

"Hey, daddy," she called out. She reached into the cooler for a Bud, and shivered as the cold air rushed around her head. "Don't you know tonight's gonna be crazy?"

* * *

June couldn't believe her dad would loan Nick the Harley. It was old, nearly as old as she was, but she sometimes thought it got better care than she did. Gabe parked the Harley in the middle of the garage, to give it lots of breathing room. He left his pickup in the driveway, where every once in a while it was rinsed by a a hard rain. Last month, some drunk had scrawled, "WASH ME YOU OLD FUCKER" in the dust on the tailgate, forcing June to take a hose to it herself.

But she saw the offer with her own eyes. After Nick's band had set up and run through a couple of songs Gabe tossed Nick the keys.

"You sure, Gabe?" he asked. He'd snatched the keys out of air, but he held his hand up, ready to throw them back.

"Course I'm sure," Gabe yelled. "But if you wreck it, I'll have a percentage of your record sales for the next ten years."

"You'll lose out on that deal," Nick said. He was gone then, the back door slamming behind him. The Harley's engine roared, and gravel splattered the wall of the building. June hurried to the front door, but all she saw in the wavy afternoon light was a line of cars waiting at the light on Lamar. Nick had vanished.

She was still standing there when Eddie pulled into the parking lot. He waved, but she pretended not to notice. She could smell the aftershave as soon as he walked in the door and made a show of fanning the air while Gabe gave them final instructions. Eddie crossed his arms over his chest and looked away from her. After Gabe was sure they were getting right to work, he winked goodbye to June and left.

"Dad's really busting his ass today, isn't he?" she said to Eddie.

He shrugged. "He's the owner." Eddie was carrying a tray of french fries to the people playing pool in the corner. The lamp over the table had been burned out for a month. It was downright dark over there, but nothing seemed to deter people bent on wasting time. Twenty-five cents to play pool, a couple of dollars for beer and hours and hours to kill.

"I need to get out of here," she told Eddie when he came back. "Think you could hold things down by yourself for a while?"

"No problem."

"Umm," she paused and moved over to give him a quick kiss. "Can I borrow your car?" His cheek was smooth. What did he need with aftershave?

"You think I'd do anything for you, don't you, June?" He sighed and handed her the keys.

* * *

They'd lived in the same brick duplex since June was a baby. Years ago, the street had been peaceful, but now it was a busy intersection. All night cars swished by outside her window, and at least once a year a drunk ran the red light and smashed into some poor soul minding his own business. Just a few months back June had awoken to a violent collision, so loud she'd sat up in bed and waited for the debris to crash through her window. When nothing came, she went to the window and stood trembling and crying as the emergency vehicles congregated. All those glowing red lights stained the street. After they'd screamed off into the darkness, she watched the traffic light swinging in the wind, changing from red to green to red. What could be easier, she thought, than stopping on red? Why did some people insist on ramming their way through life at other people's expense? Walking down the hall to her daddy's bedroom, she kept thinking about selfish people who have to have their own way. In the darkness, she felt among the rumpled sheets for him, but he wasn't there. For an instant, she wondered whether her father might have been the drunk who didn't stop on red, but it was a thought too terrible to contemplate. "I didn't see a pickup," she told herself before falling into the empty bed.

Both pickup and motorcycle were parked in the driveway when she got home. She left the Mustang by the curb and, instead of using the front door, slipped around to the side of the house and jerked the screen off her window. Going in through the window was something she'd started recently, though she wasn't sure why. Cars honked as she crawled in. Somebody yelled, but she didn't turn around. Trash, she thought, there's so much trash in this town.

Inside, she sat down on her mattress — not a real bed, just a mattress on the floor — and thought about what to do next. If she were quick, she could shower, change clothes, and leave without their knowing she'd been there, unless, of course, one of them decided to go to the bathroom, not unlikely if they were drinking beer.

When she heard the click of boots coming down the hall, June buried herself under quilts and pillows and waited. It had to be Nick: Her dad never wore anything but tennis shoes. The bathroom was right next to her room, and she could hear him unzipping, then the splash of water in the toilet. She burrowed deeper and tried to lie still when he came by again. He paused at her door before going on. In a minute, laughter drifted down the hall, and someone began picking out a tune on her dad's Martin — she knew the sound of her dad's Martin all right. June felt safe in slipping down the hall to the bathroom. Once the music started, her daddy wouldn't take the time to pee.

By the time she'd showered and dried, two guitars were going, and her daddy and Nick were singing some song she didn't recognize, Nick's most likely. June dressed to the sound of it, tying her new gray cowboy shirt up around her navel and wiggling into her oldest pair of jeans. She danced across her mattress, fluffed her hair with her hands and hoped for beauty, irresistible beauty. She'd been told once, grudgingly by her grandmother, that her momma was beautiful. And hadn't Nick so much as said that she favored her momma?

Drawn to the music, June moved up the hall, pulled by the sound to the very door of the living room. She could see Nick and her dad at the table, sitting with their chairs pushed back, feet tapping out the beat. The table was littered with empty longnecks, and the smoke of forgotten cigarettes curled and rose toward the ceiling. When they stopped, June stepped back into the shadow of the hallway.

"That's an old one," Gabe said. He propped the guitar against the wall and stood up to stretch.

"Yeah, but it's the best song you ever wrote, eh Gabe?"

"Not my song." Gabe's voice was muffled, and June figured he must have his head in the refrigerator, probably counting beers. He hated to run out, even at home.

"What do you think, I'm senile? Of course it's your song. I was there when you wrote it. For Anita. Don't lie to me."

June crept closer.

"Let's not talk about it, okay?" Gabe returned to the table with two fresh longnecks. He took a long swig of his and sat down.

"I saw her a couple of weeks back," Nick said. He got up and moved out of June's view. "Nice place you got here," he tried. Gabe didn't answer, and Nick sighed. "So, do you want to know or not?"

June thought he'd never answer. "Seems like I lie more than I tell the truth these days, but I'll try not to lie to you," he finally said. "Yeah, I want to know where she is and how she is, but I'm counting on you not to tell me." He cradled the Martin in his arms, stroking the strings then running his fingers across the wood. "She's been gone fifteen years, but sometimes I still wonder where she is and what sort of life she's living. Only now it's one stranger wondering about another stranger. I'd just as soon keep it that way. In my heart, I don't blame her for leaving me. I'm not much good, but it wasn't only me she left. What sort of woman would leave a one-year-old curly-headed baby girl with a no account like me?"

"Come on, Gabe," Nick interrupted, "give Anita hell if you want, but give yourself a break. You've done a fine job with June. She's a beautiful girl — she shines with the love you've given her."

"Well, I 'preciate your saying so, and don't get me wrong. I'm glad Anita left Junie with me. She'll never know all the happiness she turned her back on."

"No, I suppose not," Nick said quietly. In a minute, he began strumming again.

He knows where my momma is, June thought, and he thinks I'm beautiful.

"With you it's different," Gabe went on. "Music has paid off for you. You've got something to show for your life." He leaned across the table to touch his friend's arm, knocking first one empty then another to the floor.

"Ha!" Nick scoffed. "That's what you think. I've got one album to my name and a whole shitload of bills. A few more d.j.s play my songs — a few more than none — and a few women fall into my bed. That's all there is to it, Gabe."

"Hell, no, Nick!" Gabe's voice boomed.

He's getting all worked up, June thought. Her daddy was always yelling at someone — his employees, his customers, her. She'd stopped riding in the truck with him because he was always leaning out the window and yelling at other drivers. Sometimes he got into fights that way.

"You're forgetting something," Gabe continued, quieter now. "An album is something damn few of us ever get. It's a trophy, man, something you can look at and feel proud about."

"You got any trophies, Gabe? How often do you look at 'em? Sure, I woke up happy every morning for a while, but it wore off. An album's awful thin and brittle if it's all you got to show for fifteen years."

"Yeah, well," Gabe said, leaning over to collect the fallen bottles, "we all want more than we ever get, I guess."

"Stop wanting and you're probably dead." Nick agreed. "Know what I want? One more beer before it's time to face that crowd."

Suddenly, she remembered Eddie all by himself behind the bar. He'd kill her for sure if she didn't get back soon. A minute later she was crawling back out the window.

* * *

By the time she got to the Split Rail, the parking lot was jammed, and June had to park Eddie's car on the street. She knew he'd be mad; he and that car were as connected as man and machine could be. It was just an old Mustang — she'd forgotten the year, though he told her often enough. He said it was worth money, lots of money, but that sounded like her dad talking about his old Harley. June couldn't see the sense in having an old something that cost as much as a new something but broke down twice as often. Even so, she did remember to lock it, which she thought ought to count for something.

Once upon a time, the Split Rail had been a drive-in burger joint and a hang-out for teenagers. Her dad claimed he went there for root beer floats. "What's a root beer float?," she'd asked, just to rib him. The carports from those days still jutted out from the building on two sides, each one long enough to shelter a dozen cars. Now, the rickety old things served a different purpose. During breaks, customers spilled out of the hot building and lounged beneath the decaying roofs, passing joints and kissing across the darkness. After the breeze blew away the smoke and dried the sweat on their bodies they were ready to go back inside and raise some more hell.

Already, people were congregating outdoors, and as June passed, they called out and waved to her. The Split Rail had its share of regulars, most of whom made a point of calling her by name.

"Hi there," she said. She enjoyed the attention and sometimes pretended to be a famous movie star graciously acknowledging her fans. Tonight, though, she had no time to be famous.

"Where the hell have you been, June?" Eddie cried out when he saw her. He was ringing up beer with one hand and mopping up a spill on the counter with the other.

"Sorry, sorry, I got hung up, that's all." June felt more irritated than repentant. Eddie made a big deal of everything. It got old.

"So did you wreck my car or what?" he asked. The place was filling up fast. She watched while he dashed over and pulled a basket of fries from the grease. "When this batch is gone, that's it," he told her, waving his arms. "No more food."

"You can't stop serving food until nine o'clock, Eddie," she replied, taking over the register. "The sign says nine, and if you stop early, people will yell and scream."

His eyes narrowed as he slapped a plate of fries on the counter. "So what about my car, June? Is it in a ditch?"

June smirked. A balding man held out money for fries, but June ignored him. "Of course not, Eddie. Your car looks just like it did a couple of hours ago – old. I bet you can't even spot the wear and tear I put on the tires." She took the man's money then, and after ringing it into the register, called out, "put on some more fries!"

The cement floor was wet and muddy, so June took a mop from the corner and swished it around halfheartedly.

"I could use some help," Eddie said as he skidded by with a tray of food.

"This is help," she snapped. "You wanna fall on your ass?"

"I'll worry about my ass," he called over his shoulder. "You worry about a few customers."

"You sound just like my dad," June muttered. Plopping the mop in the corner, she made her way to the bar. Strictly speaking, she was only supposed to sell food and work the register. Her daddy claimed the ABC would have his license if they caught a sixteen-year-old serving beer. Still, she did it all the time and he knew it.

"What can I get you?" she asked the first customer in line, putting on her best sultry look and hoping she looked nineteen and dazzling.

By the time Nick arrived, the crowd was getting restless: they wanted to dance, to yell, and maybe even to kick ass, but, first, they needed music. When Nick walked through the front door, his hair was wet and combed back from his face. He wore a soft white western shirt with the sleeves rolled up, and the same tattered pair of Levis. June thought he looked wonderful. She handed over one last hamburger, put up the NO MORE FOOD sign, and leaned across the counter to watch him carry his guitar to the stage. As he made his way through the crowd, he smiled and nudged people aside with his guitar case. The case was patched with that gray cloth tape her dad used on everything that threatened to come apart. Nick was like her dad in that way. She knew that no matter how famous he got, he'd go on using that same old case.

Someone had left a packing crate onstage, and Nick used it for a chair, sitting down on it and opening the guitar case. The bass player, a stubby fellow with a baby face, edged over and said something. Nick sat listening and stroking the neck of the guitar.

A customer demanded her attention, then another, and by the time she'd rung up several pitchers, the band had assembled on stage.

Nick blew softly into the mike, adjusted it, then straightened and grinned at the crowd.

"Mighty fine evening, folks," he said. "I can't tell you how pleased I am to be in Austin on a night like this. Any of ya'll notice we got a great big full moon out there?"

June wanted to shout out "yes," but she knew better. Her dad had just joined her behind the bar: he was busy filling pitchers and she was ringing them up. If he thought her mind wasn't on her work, he'd keep her behind the bar all night.

"Ya'll ready for some music?" Nick cried, and the audience roared back so loudly that June dropped a customer's change, and Gabe overfilled a pitcher.

The Rail was packed. "The fire marshal'd have a heart attack," Gabe called to June over the din. People were pressed against all four walls; the waitresses had to scuttle sideways and hold their trays over their heads to get through. One gave up and started taking orders at the bar. Gabe tried to shoo her away, but she ignored him. Halfway through the first set they ran out of pitchers. Everyone was rushing headlong into a drunken stupor with Gabe helping them along as best he could. He sent June out to collect the empties. "Be careful," he called after her.

June was determined to stay out from behind the register as long as possible. She carried back several loads of pitchers then lost herself in the crowd to watch Nick. She couldn't get over how handsome he was — well, not handsome exactly. His nose was too big for handsome. Still, something about his dark eyes and pale skin — the way he held his head cocked to one side like he was trying to figure out the world — well, it was much better than simple good looks. And June wasn't the only one sighing over him. Other women were letting their beer get warm and their dates get cold.

On her next trip back to the bar, she met her dad at the sink. "Can you believe this, honey?" he asked. While his tennis shoes tapped out the beat, his hands dipped empty pitchers into an antiseptic rinse.

"Pretty crazy," June answered, handing him pitchers until he turned to her with a warm smile. "Daddy," she said, seeing her chance, "I've been working all day. When things slow down a little, during Nick's break maybe, I'm gonna take a breather."

"All right, honey," he agreed, stopping long enough to pat her shoulder with a wet hand. "Just don't leave Eddie with more than he can do."

"Miss?" a woman called from the bar. Eddie had disappeared along with the waitresses; most likely they were off in some corner smoking a joint.

"Yeah?" June said.

"A wine cooler with lime, please." The woman's voice was soft and husky.

"We don't have limes," June replied. "How about lemon?"

"All right, several slices, please." She smiled agreeably. Her hair was wild and wavy, and June, who had natural curls, suspected an expensive permanent. Nick began a new song, and the woman sighed deeply and said "Wild Horses."

"What?" June asked, passing her the wine and lemon.

The woman pressed two dollars into June's hand. "That's the name of the song," she explained. Then, as she walked away, she called out, "Keep the change."

Collecting empties, June spotted the woman under a spotlight on the edge of the dance floor. The light that shone through the sheer material of her dress revealed slender hips and legs. She was barefoot, her toenails polished a deep plum color, and she wore a silver ring on one toe. She looked out of place in the smoky, run-down bar, like someone who'd wandered in by accident. Twice before the first set ended, she returned to the bar for more wine. All that flowing hair and material made June want to spill something, so she let Eddie take the woman's orders, even though it meant losing the tips.

"What a fox," Eddie sighed.

"What a fool," June smirked.

After the first set, Nick vanished out the back door. The woman in the gauzy dress stayed inside and made small talk with the bass player, but, now and then, her eyes strayed toward the back door. June cleared the tables of cups and soggy napkins then wiped away cigarette stubs and spills with the same tired cloth. Finally, she sat down in the shadows and watched Nick reappear to claim the bass player. Absently, he draped an arm around the woman. She swayed as though to music.

"Good to see you, Jill," June heard him say.

Jill smiled and, placing a hand on either side of his head, kissed him hard on the mouth. Seeing it made June sick, but she went on watching. Nick didn't resist, but afterwards, he pulled away and bent to inspect the speakers. June took a deep breath then and walked over.

"Would you like a beer?" she asked him and felt immediately stupid. It seemed the only question she knew.

He looked up at her and brushed the damp hair from his face. "Well, June, you're a mind reader."

She flushed. "I'm a bartender."

"Aw, come on. What kind of beer do I drink?"

"Lone Star."

Nick grinned. "See there."

"Wasn't hard," June replied. "Lone Star's pretty popular around here."

Around one, business slacked off, and June took up her station on the juke box. It was one advantage of being the owner's daughter. Gabe would have run anyone else off for sitting on the juke box. "Don't you know the difference between a chair and a machine?" she could hear him saying. With her knees pressed to her chest to conceal a cup of Lone Star, she leaned against the wall and watched Nick. By now his face was red and shiny, his shirt so wet she could see the hair on his chest. Still, he looked happy to be up there sweating and singing. She smiled when he looked her way and tried not to think of all the other women doing the same. The wine coolers had finally gotten to Jill. She twirled and stretched, looking for all the world like a ballerina in a honky-tonk.

June tried to concentrate on Nick's words. He was playing her favorite song from the album. The melody washed over her, and the words left her with a pleasant ache:

Fools fall in love; wise men they fall, too.
Wise men hit the bottom, Lord, a fool just falls on through.
They fill out empty spaces like fingers fill a glove.
I must be a fool because fools fall in love.

After another song or two, the show was over. Frenzied stomping and yelling brought Nick and the band back once more, but their energy was spent. The crowd began filing out the open door, quiet and grateful for the cool night air washing over them. June finished her beer and tried to decide whether to ask Eddie for a ride home. She knew he'd want to stop off somewhere. Sighing, she wondered where all the feelings went. Just last week she was telling him what a good kisser he was.

In a few minutes only the serious drunks and newly serious couples still sat inside. June wandered out into the parking lot. Right away, she spotted Nick astride the motorcycle, his head thrown back to the stars.

"I'm looking for Pegasus. Do you see it?" he called out. June was startled.

"Are you talking to me?" she asked.

"Pegasus, the winged horse," he went on. "It's a constellation." He looked away from the stars to her face, and she had to concentrate to keep breathing.

"I don't know much about stars," she said quickly, then wished she'd lied.

"Me either. I know Pegasus, though, and I'll show you if you like."

"Sure," she said, moving toward him. She felt something open inside her as he reached for her hand and pulled her close. Blue jean against blue jean.

"Look up, Junie," Nick said, sliding a finger under her chin and gently raising her head. "There, just past my finger." He was pointing over the roof of the club and close to the horizon. She looked in the general direction, but no amount of squinting would bring those fuzzy blobs into focus. Her dad refused to buy contacts for someone who wouldn't wear glasses. She turned back to Nick. "What'd you call it again?" she asked.

"Pegasus."

"The same one as in the myths?" Finally, she'd learned something useful in school.

"The very same," he answered, then leaned back on the seat and stroked the chrome of the Harley, shiny enough to glow in the light of the moon.

"Ever seen a falling star?" June blurted out. She'd always imagined something magical, a nose-diving diamond, a streak of luck and happiness.

"More than I'd like." Nick leaned forward suddenly and gripped her shoulders, his face so close she could smell the smoke in his hair. "They come crashing down all around me, June. It's all I can do to dodge the debris." He laughed then, but his eyes were serious. When he pulled away a second later, the regret she felt was so immediate her eyes filled with tears.

"It's not hard to spot a falling star," he went on, "or even Pegasus for that matter, once you're outside the city. Out in the country, the sky is dark, and the stars shine bright and friendly. Lie still and they'll reach down and touch you."

"I've been looking for years," June said. It was true.

"Well, next time you're in the country after dark, lay down in the grass and watch the sky. If you stay put, I guarantee you your very own falling star."

June sighed. "We don't get out to the country much these days. When I was little, we used to go to my grandma's house, but now she's moved to town."

"Your daddy's momma?"

"Yes," June said, her heart beating faster. "I don't know my momma's mother or my momma, either."

"I'm sorry," Nick said, his voice suddenly flat and heavy.

"Not your fault," June said. "You know her though, don't you?" She took a breath and waited.

"Yes, I do, Junie. I've known your momma even longer than I've known your dad, and that's getting to be a long time." He smiled at her, a careful smile, then turned back to the sky.

"Could you tell me something about her?" June asked. "I was so little when she left—I really don't remember her at all."

Nick thought for a moment. "Well, would you believe she was the one who first showed me Pegasus? We were about your age, and back then, we all lived in the country. Wasn't much city to Austin in those days. One night we were fooling around with a bunch of other kids. Hell, your dad might have been with us for all I know, but that was before he and Anita noticed each other. 'Nita dragged me out into this big ole field, all tall grass and bitter-smelling wildflowers. Fireflies were buzzing everywhere. 'Nita told me when she was little she'd catch them in a jar every evening and use them as a night light. Said she'd set the jar by her bed and go to sleep by the flickering light. Then, the next morning, while everyone else was still asleep, she'd slip out in the yard in her nightgown and let 'em go. Silly, skinny girl," he said, shaking his head. "I still have a picture in my head from when she told me that. We trapped a few fireflies in our hands and studied the funny pink light coming from the cracks between our fingers. After we let 'em go, we lay down in that field, and that's when your momma astounded me. She knew every star in the heavens, June, and I thought she was about the smartest person I'd ever met. Before that night the stars were just a part of the sky for me, but since then, well, your momma showed me something that's given me many nights of pleasure."

June wanted to ask where her mother was, but she was suddenly more afraid of knowing than not knowing. By now, being in the dark was a familiar state.

The back door opened, and Jill's figure, those long limbs and that cloud of hair, were silhouetted against the light. "Nick?" she called.

"Nick?" June echoed, "if you see my momma, will you tell her I'm okay, but I miss her." She hesitated. "Does that make sense? Can you miss someone you don't know?"

"I guess you can, Junie." He leaned toward her and brushed his fingers across her cheek. She closed her eyes and sighed.

When she opened them, Jill was inching up behind him. She wanted to surprise him, but he was on to her.

"Jill, honey," Nick said quietly, "go ask Brent if he needs me to help him load the equipment."

Jill turned and hobbled back inside; as she went they heard her whisper "ouch, ouch," whenever sharp bits of gravel jabbed the soles of her feet.

"Why's she barefooted?" June asked.

Nick snorted. "Hell if I know."

"She sure is pretty."

"Is she?" Nick said.

"Definitely. Every guy in there was asking her to dance."

"Guess she looks like a lot of other women I know." He threw his leg across the cycle in one quick motion, like a cowboy slipping off a horse. "Acts like 'em too. Lot of empty people out there, June, and all of 'em lookin' for something or somebody to fill 'em up. They think music'll do it, or drinking, or fightin', or sex. So they go after it. But the next day they're still empty."

Jill appeared at the back door. "Brent said he could use some help," she called.

"All right then," he yelled to her, then turned back to June. "Just look at that moon, Junie. In your whole life you'll never see one any better than that." The moon shone right down on them, and in its bright white light, she could see his sad smile.

After he left, June went on staring at the glowing sky. She'd never felt so close to crazy. Inside, it hurt, but outside, she shivered with happiness. The only thing she wanted was Nick, Nick, Nick. She imagined running across the concrete floor into his open arms, the two of them riding away on the Harley, then her father, Eddie and Jill all waving goodbye. June could feel her face against Nick's damp shirt, and she knew how he'd smell — of sweat and smoke and something sweet.

It was all so clear that when she went inside and found the four of them sitting at a table, drinking beer and laughing, she felt she'd been tricked and had to look away as tears stung her eyes. Eddie had his apron off and was combing his hair. June ignored him. She disappeared into the cold vault and slammed the door behind her. By the time she came out, Nick and Jill were standing.

"Well folks, Jill and I are going over to the Silver Skillet for a little breakfast. Anybody wanta come along?" Nick asked.

June grabbed a rag and began wiping whatever was in reach. She didn't look up at them, but she heard the chairs scraping the floor; then Gabe ducked behind the bar and took an envelope from the metal box he usually kept in his office. It was Nick's take of the door, a fat envelope filled with small bills.

Gabe offered Nick the envelope, but Nick refused it.

"This was my pleasure, Gabe," he said. "Let's not make it business."

"What do you mean?" Gabe cried, his voice suddenly loud in the empty room. "You take this and put it toward those bills you were bellyaching about."

"I don't want the money, Gabe," Nick said quietly. "This gig was for fun; I thought you understood that."

Gabe glanced over at June, then sighed and dropped the envelope on the table. "Nick, you don't owe me a damn thing. We've avoided each other fifteen years now, two friends afraid to look one another in the eye. Well, here we are now, and I'm gonna tell it to you straight. I don't blame you. I never have, really. I don't even blame her anymore. God knows we don't pick the people we love."

June grabbed the broom and came out from behind the bar. She was intending to sweep, but the floor was already clean, so she just stood there holding the broom and looking from one man to the other.

Nick left the envelope on the table and walked away, pausing only to squeeze June's shoulder as he passed. Jill followed, carrying a purse that looked like an overnight bag. The big bag swung on her shoulder, and it knocked the broom from June's hand as she passed. Once the door closed behind them, everyone else vanished, too. The envelope was gone and so was her father. Even Eddie disappeared, but then she heard the toilet flush, and he emerged, tucking in his shirt.

She watched him step neatly over the broom, let him take her hand, and lead her to his car. He didn't ask why his car was parked on the now-empty street. Nor did he point out that the rear end jutted out a good six feet, just asking to be run into. A pretty lousy job all around, but he passed up saying so.

"You don't have to act like I'm sick or something," June said when he'd pulled away.

"You don't understand much, do you, June?" Eddie asked. She thought he was driving slow, but when she craned her neck to look at the speedometer, there was only black where the numbers should have been. What did he want with this old broken-down-heap anyway?

"Oh, I understand all right," she said. He wasn't making the turns he should have to take her home, and she was relieved not to be going there. "You think I don't?"

Until he spoke again, she was afraid. What if he'd figured it out? What if he said it out loud in the car? "I didn't get a damn bit of help with the clean up," he went on. "Your dad was in back counting his money, and you were outside flirting with a man old enough to be your father."

She let out her breath. "Oh, Eddie, for god's sake," she said. "We were looking for falling stars,"

"That's all? Haven't you ever seen one?" His voice was shrill with unhappiness, but June knew he wanted to believe her.

"No, I haven't."

"No big deal. It's like God dropping lighted matches in the dark. They go out before they touch the ground."

"Some things you want to see for yourself," she said. In the darkness, the outline of his face was like one of those black construction paper cutouts they used to make in school. "Nick said you have to go out in the country to see falling stars," she told him. They were headed out of town, climbing small hills and coasting back down, a gentle and predictable carnival ride. She didn't know where they were going, and she didn't want to know.

After a while Eddie slowed the car to a stop beside a big pasture. "Are there cows out there?" June asked. Eddie was crouched in the darkness, holding down a barbed wire fence so she could step over. "I'm afraid of cows."

"The cows are asleep, June." His voice came to her like a melody. "They never stay up late. I know that for a fact."

The weeds were high, and she was glad she was wearing jeans. Eddie held her hand, and they waded out a ways before he dropped into the grass, pulling her with him.

"You wanta see stars, June?" he asked. "I'll show you all the stars you want to see."

"Yeah?" June wondered if she'd underestimated him. Maybe he was smarter than she thought. "So where's Pegasus, if you know so much about stars?"

Eddie pointed out Pegasus and the Dippers, then some others she'd never heard of while June squinted and nodded and pretended to see. After a while, he stopped talking and leaned over to kiss first her cheeks and then her mouth. June didn't try to stop him, but she kept her eyes trained on the sky, so wide and warm and dark she could almost feel its breath.

A Simple Matter of Hunger

Last night Paul told me that loving Jancey will have to be my job. "I can't do it, Eleanor," he said. "Every time I go in and look at her, see how beautiful she is, how special, a cold wind rushes around inside me." We were in bed, and the room was so dark that I couldn't see his face. He was a voice speaking, and I was a body listening. Silent, I stared into the darkness, tried to see right through it, but the harder I looked, the thicker it got, until the darkness itself seemed to have texture, like the furry back of an enormous black bear.

In the thin hours of morning, I woke and heard Jancey rolling around in her crib. She wasn't crying, so I waited, thinking she might go back to sleep. Tiny as she is, she can make that crib creak. It's an old thing, plenty used when we bought it. Joel slept in it for nearly three years and now Jancey. Good thing she's so small, I told myself, but it's not a good thing at all.

In another minute, her crying wafted ghostlike down the hall, and before I could convince myself to throw off the covers, Paul nudged me with his knuckles. He's one of those people who can only go to sleep once each night, so he does what he can to keep from waking. Used to be, people would call in the middle of the night — broken pipes and such — and after saying hello, he'd stuff the receiver under the pillow and go right on sleeping. Eventually, we switched places. Now, I sleep closest to the phone.

The house was chilly, but Jancey's room glowed warmly. Two nightlights burned, one under the bed, and the other, a china cat, on her dresser. She wakes often, and I like to be able to change her, take her temperature even, without turning on an overhead light. Both of us stay sleepier that way. Her eyes were closed, but she was moaning and pitching from one side to the other, as though she were in the midst of a sea dream.

"Jancey," I whispered. At the sound of my voice, she opened her eyes and stared up at me, clearly awake. I hated to think of her like that, fully conscious but eyes closed. "Oh, Jancey," I said, picking her up. She was damp with sweat and so hot that I carried her across the room and switched on the light without thinking, blinding us both for an instant. I wanted to hurry her down the hall to Paul, press her close to him, wake him for good and all. Instead, I closed the door and did the only things I knew to do: I took off her sleeper and diaper, wrapped her in a blanket, coated the rectal thermometer with Vaseline, inserted it gently and sang to her while we waited.

It read 105. Drawing a deep breath, I took her into the kitchen, dribbled red liquid down her throat, and made a pact with myself. If her fever wasn't down in half an hour, I would call Dr. Kesl and have Paul drive me over to the hospital, to hell with them. As I carried her back to her room, I wondered if she could feel the pounding of my heart.

Most of her clothes were piled on the floor by the washing machine, so I put her in one of Joel's old sleepers, blue of course, but heavy and warm. She kicked her legs and stared up at me while I worked. Ordinarily, her thick black hair stands out all over her head, but last night it was slick with sweat, and after I'd dressed her, I combed the wet strands and clipped them into place with a blue barrette. "There now," I said. "You're pretty enough to go out on the town." With her dark coloring, she looks better in blue than Joel ever did.

He was a pasty little bald-headed thing, no hair on his head to speak of for over a year. "Please, God, let him have hair for a few good years," my husband Paul had prayed at the dinner table, one of those jokes that's no laughing matter. Paul's hairline has receded to the edges of his head now, nothing left but fringe around his ears and neck. He's not a vain man, but it bothers him when my hand strays to the top of his head while we make love. I like to rub the smooth skin there; something in me responds to the warm pulse beneath my fingers. I used to rub Joel's head while he nursed, my palm cupped around his skull. Love is never a pure emotion, is it? Sometimes Paul's hug brings back that sinking sensation I used to feel in the arms of my father, and once, kissing Joel goodnight, I was surprised by the same wash of tenderness that had come over me those last days with my mother in the hospital.

Jancey and I rocked for a good hour, and slowly her temperature fell. She relaxed and settled against me, her eyes opening and closing, opening again to find my face. I kept mine on her, smiled my reassurance. Once the medicine began to work, she drifted off, but as soon as I reached for the remote control to flip on the TV, she looked up at me, alert and interested. I muted the sound, but turned the chair so she could watch. She likes television — the motion and lights, the peculiar sounds. For a five-month-old, Jancey is attentive and obliging. When smiled at, she smiles; when given a toy, she holds on, waving it about with an expression that's downright grateful. If she senses she is supposed to sleep, she closes her eyes and nuzzles against me; her breathing slows. She could fool Dr. Spock with her act. We sat together and watched a couple dance across the screen, maybe Fred Astaire and Ginger Rogers. I couldn't tell for sure because I didn't have my glasses on. Their fuzzy forms swished back and forth, so graceful in the dark silence of my living room. The movie was in black and white, and it occurred to me that the dancers were probably dead, gone now except for these bits of celluloid. I went on watching until the movie was over and Jancey was deep into sleep.

* * *

Paul's side of the bed was already cold by the time the alarm went off. Up-before-he-has-to-get-up is a bad sign. When he's worried he doesn't sleep. Sometimes I find him out in the garage sweeping the cement floor, or in the back filling the bird feeder, or leaning over the fence feeding last night's bones to the neighbor's dog. This morning I found him in Jancey's room, his hands gripping the slats of her bed.

I came up behind him and rested a hand on his shoulder. "What's

131

wrong?" I whispered. All of his muscles were strung tight, and I knew that he'd have a headache in an hour or so. Believe it or not, taking in Jancey had been his idea. His brother David is a social worker for one of the state agencies here in Des Moines, and he told us all about these babies, how there's no one to take care of them. It hurt my heart to think of them. I've always been partial to babies. One night Paul told me he'd been thinking. "Don't you see?" he'd explained. "You'd have an income, and we could do a little good in this world." Doing-a-little-good runs in Paul's family. He's a plumber, but his father was a missionary, his brother's a social worker, and his mother, old as she is, volunteers three days a week at the nursing home. She told me last week she'd started a knitting group. Just yesterday she brought over three pairs of booties for Jancey. They resemble tiny Christmas stockings in odd shades of green and gold.

Jancey was sleeping, still covered with the receiving blanket I'd draped over her. She looked peaceful, but her hair was damp again. The fever was returning.

"She's getting worse, Eleanor," he said as we filed out and I closed her door.

"I'm taking her to the doctor this morning," I told him, then followed him down the hall, scuffing my big pink house slippers against the carpet. One toe was stained yellow from Jancey's vomit. I'd washed the shoe in the sink, but the worst things, the things you don't want to be reminded of, those never come out. While I watched my slippers take one step at a time, I thought of those dancers, the way they'd seemed to float, the woman's dress billowing, nothing in the world to hold her down.

Paul put on the coffee and kept his back to me. First thing in the morning he walks around the house in boxer shorts. The material flaps around his spindly legs, and his long pale feet slap at the floor. He's a strong man in most ways, but what drew me to him, what keeps me close now, are his weaknesses. While he waited for the water, he went down the hall to give Joel his first shaking. Five or six times each morning Paul or I pull off the covers and shake Joel's foot, each time harder than the last. Joel is six years old now, but he still hasn't discovered anything he likes better than sleeping. This morning Paul tried tickling, and it seemed to work. I could hear Joel's desperate little giggle, then a breathless "Stop, Dad, stop."

The coffee was ready by the time he got back. "A new technique?" I asked, trying to keep my voice light. He filled his cup slowly then turned to me. His skin was still baggy from sleep, and he looked old. He'd been in there tickling Joel, but there was no trace of a smile on his face. "You knew it was going to be like this, didn't you?" I asked. His hand trembled a little as he replaced the pot.

"God knows I didn't," he said simply. Then he carried his coffee away down the long hall to the bathroom.

* * *

The pediatric waiting room is divided into two unequal sections by a length of Plexiglass that juts out into the middle of the room. A table at one end keeps people from walking into the flat edge. Orange and brown upholstered chairs line both sides of this transparent wall, back to back, as though some enormous game of musical chairs is about to begin. The smaller section of the room is reserved for well patients, and a prominent sign directs the rest of us to the other side.

When I carried Jancey in this morning, I stopped in the entranceway, momentarily confused. Some redecorating had gone on since our last visit. A large oval braided rug covered an expanse of institutional carpet in the unwell section, and a baby not much older than Jancey was seated in the big middle of it. While I watched, he crawled to the edge then back again, as though the rug were an island and he were marooned.

"Come on in," one of the receptionists called to me, waving and smiling in that way teachers and nurses and social workers do, professional encouragers.

I had Jancey in her big plastic carseat. It's shaped something like a bucket or a scoop and is perfectly portable if you're big and strong. The inside was lined with receiving blankets, and Jancey was asleep among them. She'd slept straight through her morning feeding, and when I'd lifted her from the crib into the seat she hadn't so much as stirred. More than once this morning I'd passed my hand before her face to feel her breath. When I got to the counter, I heaved the seat onto it and sighed in relief. The three receptionists who work the desk dress in nurses' uniforms, but to assert their individuality, they also wear sweater vests or buttondowns in bright primary colors. They're trim and efficient and seem always to have gotten enough sleep the night before.

The blonde curly-haired one ran a finger down a list of appointments until she found the name then glanced up at me and smiled brightly.

"Jancey Hernandez," she said, her voice much louder than it needed to be. Instantly, the other two looked up. One was on the phone, the receiver cradled on her shoulder, and the other was seated in front of the computer, watching as one screen after another clicked past. The one at the computer abandoned her post to come over.

"I never pass up a chance to coo at a baby," she explained to no one in particular. Her red hair was clipped short around her ears and neck but had been left fluffy on top; little tendrils curled prettily. On her blue sweater she wore a puffy plastic heart pen, red as Snow White's apple. Last month she'd sported a snowman with a tiny top hat, and the month before that a fat Jack O'Lantern. I'd seen her many times in the last few months, watched her fingers moving over the keys of the computer, her small perfectly shaped head bent to the task. She'd never taken notice of me or my baby.

"What a darling," she cried, peering into the bucket from a safe distance. I stared back and said nothing.

"Dr. Kesl will be with you shortly, Mrs. Wilson," the blonde told me as she, too, moved closer to get a look at my baby. I was grateful Jancey was sleeping; otherwise, I knew she would smile back at them, betraying us both. Grabbing up the bucket, I turned and made my way across the brief expanse of carpet to the first available seat. I sat down just as my arms began to shake.

Of course, a baby with AIDS is the sort of thing people talk about, but I hadn't expected it from the people at the Clinic. Up until now, we'd kept the secret fairly well, I'd thought, the doctors, Paul, and I. By some sort of unspoken agreement, we rarely use identifying terms, referring only occasionally to "the disease." Otherwise, we talked about the same illnesses that worry other parents: ear infections, staph infections, urinary infections. For Jancey though, these diseases are only symptoms, not the real thing. Sometimes, I think of AIDS as a monster, the kind that lives in closets in children's books, a horrifying creature with five heads, a scaly body, and horns growing out of his tail. The more frightened I become, the bigger and uglier he gets, until I am sure that he will burst out of the closet and kill us all.

After I'd recovered, I settled Jancey's seat into the chair next to mine and pulled the covers from around her so she wouldn't get too hot. Revived by the cool air of the waiting room, she began the slow process of waking, a series of stretches, blinks, and yawns. Like Joel, she is more at home in her dream world than in this one.

The receptionists made a pretense of returning to work, but again and again their eyes strayed to Jancey. While they watched, I raised her from the bucket and into my arms, bent my face to hers and kissed the round apple of her cheek. When I felt the warmth of her skin against my lips, my heart shrank back. I've never been afraid of Jancey before, not even that first time I held her in the hospital, when the nurse had lifted her into my arms and said, "She's yours now. God bless you." To stop it, to reprimand us all, I spoke aloud: "She's just a baby, damn it."

Only the curly-haired receptionist seemed to hear. She looked over at me as though I were a new arrival, someone she hardly recognized. "Is Jancey here today for a routine checkup, Mrs. Wilson?" she asked, her eyes flitting to a spot on the wall just above my head and then back to my face again. Obligingly, I craned my head to read the sign: THIS SECTION RESERVED FOR WELL PATIENTS ONLY. YOUR COOPERATION IS APPRECIATED. Smiling, I turned back to her. "Yes," I lied, suddenly myself again.

Jancey and I sat and played pat-a-cake for five minutes or so, until she wet her diaper. While we were off in the restroom changing it, another mother arrived with her baby, a red and shriveled newborn. Though the room was full of empty chairs, the mother took the seat right next to mine. Perhaps she noticed Jancey's empty baby bucket and imagined we might have a chat.

No big deal, really, her sitting next to us. Such a thing might have happened anywhere else, and I wouldn't have given it a thought. Jancey couldn't give her illness to either the mother or her child — even the receptionists knew as much. Still, their foreheads furrowed with concern. "All right," their expressions said. "You've made your point. Now get back to the sick section where you belong." And I considered doing just that — gathering my things, and murmuring some sort of excuse, something about a sneeze or a cough. But I couldn't do it. People who've lost control of life are a superstitious lot: they look for signs, indulge in rituals, refuse to backtrack or take peeks into the future. They huddle in the present and hold on for dear life. It seemed a bad move to go from the well section to the sick section, hasty and unnecessary. So I stayed put and smiled graciously at the new mother, dressed just as I was in the housewife uniform of blue jeans and plain-front sweatshirt, hers powder blue and mine Christmas green.

Jancey rested on my chest, her head on my shoulder. The waving and cooing she'd done while I changed her diaper were over. She seemed spent, her limbs slack, as though she were sleeping. Periodically, though, I felt the brush of her lashes against my neck. I sighed deeply, prompting the new mother to touch my arm. "It's tough, isn't it?" she said.

Her baby was tucked into the small valley between her legs, swaddled hospital fashion. Seeing him reminded me of the day I'd brought Joel home from the hospital. Anxiously, I'd unwrapped him to check his diaper then been unable to rewrap him again. Poor thing, he'd spent an hour or more on the kitchen table wailing and kicking, so angry and frightened that he finally lay gasping for breath while I rolled him up first one way, then another. By the time I gave up, I'd been crying, too. I remembered it now as though it had happened to someone else.

"Yes, it is," I replied, and while I watched, the little being in the blue blanket began to struggle, rocking himself in his mother's lap like an upended and legless caterpillar, helpless, entirely so.

"Hungry again?" his mother asked him, as though all unhappiness were a simple matter of hunger. Already an old hand, she leaned over her diaper bag, drew forth a crocheted blanket, draped it over one shoulder, and lifting the sweatshirt beneath it, readied herself to nurse. Her baby had just opened his mouth to wail when she turned his body and gently nudged his head beneath the green and yellow crochet. I watched him latch on then relax against her.

"Are you nursing?" the new mother asked, ready now for our chat. I had already decided to say yes. After all, I had nursed Joel for nearly a year. Just watching her brought back the ache of the milk followed by the pull of the baby's mouth, pain that passed into pleasure.

"Jancey Hernandez," the nurse called out. I lurched to my feet, jerking Jancey so that her head banged against my shoulder. She responded with a one syllable scream, a sound like someone falling down a well. The new mother looked up at me, surprised. Her baby lay nestled against her, both of them in exactly the right place. For them, this visit to the doctor would be nothing more than an exchange of smiles and compliments. Afterwards, they'd go home and nap together, still nearly one.

* * *

I'd been home from the clinic for maybe fifteen minutes when I spotted Joel from the kitchen window, on his way home for lunch. He trudged slowly up the sidewalk, hands in his pockets, a red wool cap pulled low over his forehead. As I watched, he smiled to himself, and my heart lifted, but the smile faded quickly. As he approached the house, Joel seemed to grow smaller instead of larger. I turned away from the window and set his place for lunch, resisting the impulse to rush out and hug him tight. I'd whipped up a box of macaroni and cheese, opened a couple of cans — green beans and fruit cocktail. I arranged several spoons of each on a plastic plate and stored the rest in the refrigerator.

"Where's your lunch?" he asked when he came into the kitchen. Usually, we sit down to lunch together.

"Shh," I said, "Jancey's sleeping."

The doctor's office had sapped whatever energy she had left. The mere sight of someone in white terrifies her. To Dr. Kesl and the others, she's a tiny hostile being, stiff and red-faced. Her rage, though I've seen it many times, surprises even me. In the car on the way home from these visits, she wails, gathers her breath, then wails again. To calm her, I sing lullabies as I drive, my voice so loud that by the time we turn into the driveway, both of us are hoarse. Once, Paul rode

137

along, and was shocked by the din we created. "Eleanor," he cried, "you're screaming, too." On the way home today, I gave up the pretense of singing and simply screamed along with her. At a red light, I paused for breath, and turning my head, looked out the window. In the car next to me an elderly woman sat watching, one hand over her mouth. Snapping my own mouth closed, I tried to compose my features, to reassure her with a smile, but she wouldn't look my way again. She sat stiffly in her bucket seat, staring through her windshield. When the light changed, she pulled away fast, as though leaving the scene of a crime.

"What did the doctor say?" Joel asked. He sat down and picked up his fork.

"Oh, not much new," I sighed, striking that delicate balance between near-truth and outright lie. Joel knows a little about Jancey, but not as much as he should know.

"Jancey's sick, you know," I said, sitting down next to him.

He turned to me with those gentle eyes of his, my mother's eyes. "Don't worry, Momma," he said, patting my knee. "She'll get better." My words, he consoled me with them now.

"Do you think so?" I asked. Then, I got up to fix him a glass of milk.

* * *

"Be prepared," Dr. Kesl had told me. "She may take a turn for the worse." He'd examined her slowly — pressing, tapping, prodding — his big hands passing over her again and again. I stood by silently, my eyes on his face, trying to guess his thoughts. No point in asking questions. Jancey's piercing cry drowned out everything, even the ringing telephone. The nurse, who slipped in and out of the room while Dr. Kesl worked, stuck her hand in the door at one point and waved a slip of paper. ANSWER THE PHONE, it said in large red letters.

Dr. Kesl had seemed distracted in a way I couldn't interpret. Something was worrying him, but it might have been something other than Jancey. "Everything doesn't have to do with you," my mother used to remind me.

"Listen," I said when he'd finished the exam, shouted his directions, and passed on a new sheaf of prescriptions. He was stripping off the gloves while his nurse ripped the paper from the examining table. Both of them wore masks and paper gowns; I felt like a naked person on a spaceship. Dr. Kesl glanced over at me and moved to the sink, thrust his hands beneath the faucet and began to wash in that way they all learn in medical school. "Don't adoptive mothers nurse sometimes?" I asked him. I was dressing Jancey, pushing her thin brown arms into the sleeves of a yellow playsuit. Because Dr. Kesl no longer loomed over her, she screamed intermittently. We talked in the silent spaces she left us.

"They do, yes," he replied, half-turned away, clean and ready to go. Dr. Kesl is a tall man with permanently hunched shoulders and a small bald patch on the back of the head that should make him look older but somehow doesn't. Seeing it made me think of the little bald spot newborns get from rubbing their heads against the sheet. I used to like Dr. Kesl very much. "Don't know much about it, though," he finished and went out the door. As soon as he was gone, Jancey quieted, a momentary lull. I could feel her eyes on my face, but I didn't look back at her just yet. Instead, my gaze slipped from the dark wood of the closed door over to a matted and framed photo of a waterfall that hung between the door and one corner of the wall. Dr. Kesl had snapped it himself while vacationing in Hawaii. I remembered the day he'd pointed it out to me, a better day for both of us. "You ought to go sometime," he'd suggested, his smile warm on me. I'd nodded and cradled newborn Jancey, who still trusted doctors and lay quietly in my arms.

This afternoon, the photograph seemed changed; I no longer recognized its contours. I blinked and stared, blinked and stared, but what I saw made no sense to me. It might have been abstract art. Backing up to a chair, I sank into it and turned my eyes to Jancey. She waited for me in her bucket, intent on a mobile that hung over the examining table. Little lambs, pigs, and rabbits turned slowly above our heads. When the nurse looked in, we were both watching the animals. "Are you all right, Eleanor?" she asked. I noticed for the first time that she, too, was wearing a puffy heart pin. Coincidence, I told myself, though I no longer believe in it.

* * *

After Joel returned to school, I flipped on the TV and sat down to watch my soap. I remember nothing of what I saw, though I stared at the screen, my hands folded in my lap. Halfway through the program, I got up and hurried back to the bedroom to Paul's desk. One of the drawers is reserved for my things — old letters, Joel's baby book, a box so full of Mother's costume jewelry that I keep it closed with rubber bands. In the manila folder marked JANCEY I found the letter I received a few weeks ago. The envelope is lavender, postmarked San Antonio, Texas. Holding it, I thought of pictures I've seen of the Alamo, a small fort surrounded by palm trees, the hot sun beating down on people wearing big straw hats.

Jancey's mother is a young woman, hardly more than a teenager. If the picture she sent favors, she is pretty. Her dark hair waves over her shoulders, full and soft looking, but her bangs are teased and sprayed, so that she looks as if she's just come in out of the wind. Her features are arranged neatly on her face; nothing calls attention to itself. The photo she sent, which was taken in one of those arcade booths, is actually a series of three photos. She must have sat very still while the camera clicked because all three look remarkably the same. On the back, she scrawled, TO ELEANOR, WITH LOVE FROM MARY ELIZABETH. You'd think I were her aunt or some school friend. Actually, Mary Elizabeth and I have never met. In some ways, she is no more real to me than the characters on my show. None of them has AIDS, but several have drug problems. They prick their arms with needles and take hideous chances in dark corners. Like her, these characters are young and carry their problems home to their parents. When Mary Elizabeth got sick, she moved back to her mother's house in San Antonio. In her letter, she described cramped quarters and her mother's habit of cooking more food than the two of them can possibly eat. "P.S." she wrote, "Please call me sometime," but she didn't include her phone number.

"She doesn't really want you to call," Paul told me when I wondered about it out loud.

"Maybe she just forgot," I said.

She had printed her address in the upper left-hand corner of the envelope, so it was a simple matter of calling directory assistance. Someone answered on the fourth ring.

"Hello," I chirped, my voice falsely cheerful, like some salesperson's. "This is Eleanor Wilson. Is Mary Elizabeth there?"

"No, she's not." A mixture of accents gave the words a rich, rounded sound, but I heard the hesitancy behind them. This was Mary Elizabeth's mother, Jancey's grandmother. I tried to think what she might look like. Dark hair and dark eyes was as far as I could get.

"Mrs. Hernandez," I went on. "I'm Eleanor Wilson, Jancey's foster mother. Mary Elizabeth sent me a letter a few weeks ago. She asked me to call."

All I heard was her breath, then mine, then hers again. "My baby Jancey?" she finally murmured.

"Yes," I said.

"Do you know I've never seen her, Mrs. Wilson? Only photos and those are months old."

"Well, I could send..."

"No, don't," she interrupted. "It's good of you, but sometimes it's easier not to believe in her, not to believe in any of it."

"She's real, Mrs. Hernandez," I said quietly.

"To you she's real," the rich voice came back. "To me, Mary Elizabeth is real. When you called, I was putting on my sweater, going out the door. She's in the hospital. They don't say when she might come out."

"Oh," I sighed.

"I pray for you every day," Mrs. Hernandez told me. Her voice was suddenly thin. It hardly reached my ear before it was gone.

I thanked her. In the other room, the crib creaked as Jancey shifted and stretched. In another minute or so, I knew she would begin to sob.

"Do you believe in God, Mrs. Wilson?" Mary Elizabeth's mother asked. My own mother had asked the same question of me the day before she died.

"I try." It was the answer I'd given Mother, though not the one she'd hoped for. The last time I'd bent to kiss her, she'd thrown her arms around me, clutched at me as though she expected us to be separated for eternity. "Listen," I said, then stretched my arm overhead, holding the receiver into the air. Jancey was wailing; her indignant scream grew louder each time she took a breath.

"Oh, my little baby," I heard Mrs. Hernandez say.

* * *

By the time I hung up, Jancey had soaked herself, her blankets, the sheet. While I cleaned up the mess, I spoke to her in that funny, high-pitched voice she likes.

"Guess who was on the phone?" I asked. She gazed up at me intently. As usual, I had her undivided attention. "Your grandmother," I went on. "You didn't even know you had a grandmother, did you? And she loves you. We all love you."

When she was clean, I carried Jancey into my bedroom, sat down with her in the rocker by the window and put her to my breast. She seemed to know what to do. She sucked for a moment, looked up at me, then returned to the task. She will get nothing today, I know, but if we keep it up, my body may respond.

The view from this window is the best in the house. From my chair, I can see a line of farmland—tan in winter and green in summer—and above that, a wide swatch of sky. Birds glide by, soaring then dipping out of sight. When I was a little girl someone told me that birds house the souls of the dead. I don't know who would tell a child a thing like that, but the idea has stuck with me. I remember being eight years old and standing stock still in the fields, shading my eyes with one hand so I could watch those birds move back and forth between heaven and earth. It seemed to me then that they couldn't quite decide which place they liked best. Sometimes, I tried to sneak up on them while they pecked at the ground. "It's all right," I'd whisper when I got close. "I just want to know your name." Of course, the sound of my voice sent them straight back to the skies. Startled souls, they have always been just out of my reach.

Happiness Tricks

I'm all by myself when they come in, a little boy and his mother, both of them dragging pillowcases stuffed with dirty clothes. Right away, the little boy reminds me of somebody, but I can't think who it is.

"Can I have a can of pop?" this boy asks. He might be four, and he has one of those screechy little voices that get on your nerves.

"No." The answer comes so quick it must've been loaded and waiting in the back of his mother's mouth.

The boy sidles over to the soda machine and tries the buttons while his mother yanks clothes from pillowcases and restuffs them into the nearest machine.

They don't notice me over on the other side of the room, sitting in chair number fourteen if you start to the right of the front door. Lately, I can't stop counting things. Thirty-nine people on the bus today. Thirty chairs in this laundromat, fifteen washers and twelve dryers, not much bigger than the one in our apartment building at home.

The boy's on his tiptoes, punching and repunching the buttons he can reach. After a minute, he bends over and peers into the hole, checking for cans. Nothing. To make sure, he reaches inside and feels. His hair is flaming red, long and curly. He's wearing overalls too small, and his T-shirt is on backwards—the tag wags out at his neck like a little tongue. When he bends over, I recognize that creamy, see-through skin at the back of his neck. My sister Peggy has skin like that. Sometimes, when I'm braiding the thin plait of hair that falls between her shoulder blades, I touch her neck with the tips of my fingers. Every time, she shudders and tucks her head like a duck.

Peggy's different from the rest of our family. She wears lace and black flats and is forever rising onto her toes. Even though she's twelve and still hasn't had a single lesson, she believes in her heart that she was born to be a ballet dancer. It's on her mind all the time. When I wake up in the mornings, she's there by the window, stretching and twirling, that dreamy expression on her face.

Our daddy gets that expression, too, mostly when he talks about the past. Once upon a time, Daddy played bass in a rock band, and the year he was fifteen—my age exactly—he hitchhiked to Woodstock to shake Jimi Hendrix's hand. That's his favorite story, mine too. I know it by heart. Momma snorts when she hears it, says he lifted everything he knows about Woodstock from the movie. "Fat chance your daddy could've found his way from Jackson, Mississippi to Woodstock, New York," she says. "That man can't drive across town without getting lost."

He does have a lousy sense of direction. Twelve whole years in Dallas, and he didn't learn the first thing about the highway system. After the divorce, he was even worse. One Sunday he came over to take Peggy and me to the zoo. We spent two hours getting there, one hour looking at the animals, and two hours finding our way home. That's why we didn't blame him for moving back to Jackson. It's where he grew up; he has a map of the town in his head.

"Roy, go get the soap out of the backseat," calls the mother. She's wearing a no-nonsense expression, like he better hurry up and do as she says.

He takes one last look at the soda machine and heads for the door. Satisfied, his mother fishes quarters out of her sweater pocket and fits them into the slots. She looks bored or tired or maybe both.

144

She has her back to the window, so she can't see Roy yanking on the back door of the old barge. Barge is my dad's name for those enormous old gas guzzlers people used to drive. This one is as big as a house and old—so old. One of the headlights is smashed, and the front hood is buckled. Probably makes loud, embarrassing noises as it waits in line with other cars. I've always felt sorry for kids that have to ride in barges. My parents drive old cars, but at least they get 'em small and quiet. When Dad left for Jackson, he was driving a white Toyota with a blue hood.

I watch as Roy steps onto the sidewalk with a huge open box of detergent clasped to his chest. I hold my breath and hope he doesn't fall. In my mind I see him tripping and hitting the pavement, the soap arcing out of the box in a long white curve. But it doesn't happen. He gets to the door just fine, puts the box down, and presses his weight against the glass. Nothing. He tries again. I look around for his mother, who's disappeared. Must be in the bathroom. Roy's got his back to the glass, pushing with all his might. Just above his head a sign reads PULL. I go over, tap on the glass, and wait for him to look around. His face is puzzled and a little red. Opening the door a crack, I tell him to move back. "The box, too," I add, motioning with the back of my hand.

"Oh yeah," he mutters. He's an easy kid, the kind you like to babysit.

When I open the door, the night air rushes in, cool and wet. Roy edges past with his box of soap. He's careful, but he still manages to stomp on one of my toes.

"Where's your shoes?" he asks me, putting down the box.

"In the washer," I say.

When the Greyhound left Dallas this morning, it was raining. All afternoon the bus drove through one continuous storm. By the time we pulled into Jackson, the rain had stopped, but water was standing everywhere. Soon as I got off the bus I stepped splat into a mud puddle. Like a little kid or something.

My machine is in the spin cycle, rumbling and bucking like a live thing. I go over and press my palms against the lid to feel the vibrations. "You will have a very happy life," I tell myself.

By the time it stops, Roy's back at his station, punching the NEHI grape button over and over. Everytime he reaches for the button, those overalls hike up between his legs. Poor kid.

Soon as I dump my tennis shoes and socks in the dryer, I go over and take a seat in number twenty-four, right across from the soda machine. The bathroom door is still shut tight, and the detergent box is right where Roy left it. By now, his mother's washers are agitating to beat the band.

"How old are you?" I ask Roy.

"Four," he answers, holding up his fingers. "How old are you?"

"Fifteen." I hold out both hands and one foot, wiggle my toes and smile. I've been babysitting every weekend for the past three years, but no kid's ever asked *my* age before. I wish Peggy could meet this one.

Wishing does it, brings on that falling sensation, like someone's just tossed me off a cliff. I grip the seat and wait for it to pass, tell myself it must be what Alice felt when she drifted down the rabbit hole, falling and not knowing if it'll ever stop.

Daddy made a point of reading us *Alice in Wonderland*. "I've always identified with the Cheshire Cat," he explained, that crazy grin on his face. Momma hated that smile, said it made him look like Jack Nicholson. But Peggy kept him going. She painted poster-boards to look like playing cards and tied them together at her shoulders with hair ribbons. Weekends, she'd parade around the house in them. "I wish I could really be there, Mona," she'd say. "I don't even think I'd wanta come back."

Roy comes over and touches my knee. "One time that machine gave me a Seven-Up," he says.

"For free?"

He nods solemnly.

"Just luck," I tell him. "The machine must've been broken or something." I reach in my pockets, finger my quarters, and eye the bathroom door. Suppose the woman never comes out? Will I have to call the police? Take Roy with me? Break down the door? "Here," I tell him, pressing the coins into his small palm. "You have to pay for things."

Roy hurries over to the machine. I lift him up and wait while he feeds it quarters. "Okay," I tell him. "Try your button now."

He does, and the miracle happens: his can drops into the hole. Turning to me, Roy squeals and claps his hands.

"All right," I say. "Way to go."

He needs my help to open it, and while he takes his first sip, I work at the straps of his overalls. The cloth is stained with rust and doesn't want to give. I have to tug and fiddle, but Roy stands still.

"I like Pepsi," Roy tells me.

"What's your mother doing?" I ask when I've made a little progress on the straps. He frowns then shrugs. I know what he's feeling. Parents are so secretive, always scuttling into bedrooms and locking doors. Speaking in whispers and turning their faces away. Maybe we start with our own secrets just to be like them. I didn't tell a soul I was leaving home, not even Peggy.

When I'm done with Roy's straps I pat his shoulders. "Soon as my shoes are dry, I'm going to see my father." I want to tell someone.

"Me, too." His face is solemn, and he holds the can of Pepsi to his chest. For a second I think he means he's going with me, and I picture the scene — Roy and me knocking at my daddy's front door.

"Are you talking about your dad?" I ask. He nods, and the long red curls on the top of his head move slowly, like the antennae of a small bug. His hair is golden red and full of light, but it's so long people probably mistake him for a girl.

"Sometime I am," he goes on. "And he's gonna take me for a ride in a rocket."

Roy makes a takeoff noise and lifts the Pepsi can toward the ceiling.

"Really?" I think of Peggy and all those ridiculous stories she tells me, stuff she reads in *The National Enquirer:* a boy who lives inside a pumpkin, and a woman who's married to a creature from outer space. Talking babies and old men who fly with the birds. She believes every bit of it. "Anything can happen," she says, that dreamy expression on her face.

For a second, I'm about to cry. So, I close my eyes and listen to my breath, a happiness trick my daddy taught me. After a while I notice Roy's mother's clothes are spinning; then the machines click to a stop. "Your momma's clothes are done," I tell Roy, thinking they're not clean because she didn't use any soap.

"Oh!" Roy hurries over to the bathroom door, knocks once, and calls "Momma" in a grown-up sounding voice. After a second, a puff of hair appears through a crack in the door; then, his mother emerges. She's carrying an old magazine in one hand, and she goes on clutching it while she empties the washers into a wire cart and pushes the cart, full to overflowing, toward the row of dryers. Everything in her pile is some subtle shade of the same color, a pinkish gray. She passes right by me, but I might as well be a ghost.

She doesn't notice Roy's can of Pepsi, either. My mother would have been asking a whole slew of questions: "Where'd you get that Pepsi-Cola, Ramona?" Her voice rings in my head, but after only a day, I can't call up her face.

Instead, I look at Roy's mother's face. Hers is younger than my mother's with a little bulb of a nose and eyes that sag slightly at the corners. She's wearing green and brown – baggy, dreary-looking clothes – but I notice a flash of red nails as she grabs handfuls of wet clothes. Once the dryers are going, she finds a blue chair at the other end of the room and reopens her magazine.

Roy plays with his empty can. He rolls it down the long aisle between the washers and dryers then scoots after it on his stomach, marine-style. The child is a human mop. When he passes my chair, I bend down and run my fingers through his curls. A girl should be blessed with his head of hair. If he were a girl, I could do something cute with it, but on him it's always gonna be a waste. Before he slides away, Roy looks back at me, and I notice his eyes are green, my favorite color. The hair and the eyes, they must've been gifts from his father. Everyone in my family has flat, brown eyes, ordinary, all of us perfectly ordinary.

Suddenly, I feel tired. All I want to do is stretch out across a row of chairs. I'm not planning on sleeping, just a little rest, but once I find a comfortable fit, I doze right off. Of course, I have one of those crazy dreams that seem terrible when you're asleep and funny when you wake up. Something about running barefoot down the streets of Jackson, turning here and there, no idea where I'm going. Mother and Peggy are right behind me – throwing tennis shoes and calling me names.

I jerk up, scared. The laundromat's so quiet my breathing's all I can hear. I expect Roy to be gone, but he's over in chair number four, his mother in number six. The wire basket, heaped with dry clothes, stands between them. Roy's mother folds while Roy stuffs the folded clothes into a pillowcase. He goes about the task with a vengeance – hammering the pillowcase with a fist to make more room. His mother stares out at the empty parking lot.

My shoes are dry. I put them on and go back to the seat where I stowed the purple and pink nylon bag. Peggy bought it for her ballet classes, so of course it's never been used. All at once, I realize how wrong it was of me to take it. Now, it'll never be Peggy's dance bag. Now, it'll always be the bag Ramona used to run away.

Roy gets tired of hammering clothes and wanders over in my direction. I wish I could sit him on my lap, but I make do with touching his sleeve. He waits beside me like a dog with a big heart. I had a dog like that once. He just appeared one Sunday afternoon, climbed up on the porch and and heaved a big sigh. About a year later he moved on. I still remember his name – Sandy – and the way he curled up to sleep at night with his head resting on his tail.

"You have a dog, Roy?" I ask. A dog would be just the thing for him.

He shakes his head then adds, "I might get me one sometime." We both look down at the linoleum, concentrate on his small black hightop sliding back and forth. Sooner or later it happens: he slips and the bottom of his dirty sneaker rubs the top of my clean one. I feel him stiffen.

"It's all right," I whisper. "You have brothers and sisters?"

Roy shakes his head.

"I have a sister named Peggy."

"Where is she?" Roy asks, looking around. I imagine Peggy's head popping up from behind a washer and her voice, "Wanna see my new step?" I can almost see her then, pirouetting down the aisle.

"She's in Dallas," I say to both of us.

"Oh yeah," Roy nods. "My daddy lives there." I don't answer. Instead, my fingers search out the tiny pocket between the bones in Roy's elbow, and I listen to my breath until I can smile again.

"I think I better go," I say and grab up Peggy's bag.

Once I'm outside I figure I'll know what to do, but it doesn't happen that way. To the right, to the left, in front of me, behind me? I have no idea which way to go. Beyond the parking lot is the highway the bus came in on. An overpass stretches up into the black sky like the back of some enormous cat. Across the street, the lights of a filling station push back the night, but all the other buildings huddle in the dark, closed and empty.

In a minute, Roy and his mother come out. Roy's carrying the soap again, and his mother lugs two pillowcases jammed with those pinkish-gray clothes. She opens the back door, tosses in her load and goes back for the rest. If she sees me standing there, she gives no sign. "Off with her head," I mutter.

Roy leaves the box on the sidewalk and hops into the backseat. In a minute, I see him climb into the front. Behind me, his mother shoulders her way out the door. Gathering my courage, I move toward the box of soap, pick it up, and follow her to the car.

"My father lives at 3510 Robinson Street," I say. "Do you know where that is?"

She hesitates. For a second, I wonder whether she'll ignore me even now. Then she turns and gives me a long look. "Yeah, I know," she says.

"Uhh, I just got to town, and I don't know my way around. What I was wondering is if maybe . . . I could get a ride?"

"What's wrong with your dad? Can't he come get you?"

"Well, he doesn't really know I'm here."

She cocks her head. From the corner of my eye I see Roy's face shining out of the darkness of the car.

"You run away from home, didn't you?" she asks.

"Not really," I say, "I'm here to see my dad." Does that count? Is it running away if you're going to see a blood relative?

"I run away when I was your age," she tells me. "Didn't get me anywhere though." She looks down and notices the box of soap. "Where are you going with my soap?"

"I'm bringing it to the car for you," I snap, my voice a little smart-alecky, like I was talking to my own mother. So I add, "Just trying to help."

"All right, then. Get in."

"Thank you very much," I say.

No one talks in the car, not even Roy. His mother navigates the barge down streets so quiet and still you'd think it was the middle of the night. In a few minutes, we drift to a stop.

All this time I've been imagining my daddy coming and going from an apartment. Nothing big or fancy, maybe one of those square buildings with the front doors that face a small pool. But 3510 Robinson is an old white frame house, the kind of place you picture for a grandmother—cats perched on porch railings and sidewalks crumbling out front. I can just hear what my mother would say: "I ain't got much, Ramona, but I do have a few standards and central air is one of them."

"This it?" Roy's mother asks.

"Guess so," I say and open the door. I get out with my bag then put my head back in. "I 'preciate your bringing me," I tell her and turn to Roy. "Bye, Roy."

"Bye, bye," he says softly. "Thank you for the Pepsi."

"You're welcome." I want to say something else, something special for him to remember me by, but I can't think what it would be. So I just touch his curls and wave as they drive away. When they're gone, I feel as though I've lost my family. I have to remind myself that my dad is just a few feet away.

The front steps are rickety, and I can't find the doorbell in the dark. I run my hand across the wood until the grit of peeling paint is under every fingernail. All the while, something inside of me is growing, pushing at my lungs so I can hardly breathe.

"Daddy, Daddy, let me in!" I finally scream, and I pound the screen with my fists.

The door opens right away, and a woman peers out. I step back and stare at her. She's tall and thin, and she sways a little as she stands there, like the wind is blowing against her.

"I . . . I thought James Oatney lived here," I say.

"Jimmy!" she calls, and in a second, I see him behind her.

"Mona?" His face comes close. I remember his voice now, and the way he bends over to talk to me, like I was still a little girl. "What're you doing here?"

"I came for your birthday," I tell him.

"Mona," he says again. Putting an arm around me, he guides me over to the stairs. "Here, let's sit down for a minute."

"'Member when you went to Woodstock?" I ask when I'm calm enough to talk.

"Woodstock?" It's that woman behind us. She says the word like she doesn't recognize it, like it doesn't mean a thing to her.

I want to ask Daddy whether he got lost on the way, whether he met people he loved and never saw again. But I take one breath, then two, and I don't say anything at all. Instead, I think about Jimi Hendrix, gone so long now he might as well be a creature from Alice's Wonderland. In pictures he looks so serious, but Daddy said he smiled at Woodstock. From my seat on the porch, I can almost see him, or at least I can see his face, a dark moon hovering high above us.

Learning to Dance

I have a brand new stainless steel mixing bowl, big enough for a baby to swim in. I'm glorying in the shiny professionalism of it, thinking how much easier it will be to mix one large batch rather than several small ones. The hunks of cream cheese warm on the counter; in July it doesn't take long for them to soften. I drop egg after egg into my big, beautiful bowl. The yolks drift in the bottom like lily pads on a pond, and as I stand watching them, I begin to sweat. It's only been half an hour since I got out of the shower, but already I feel like climbing back in. Why didn't Momma put in central air conditioning, I ask myself for the first time today. Instead, she bought these damn window units that I can't afford to run. They're stuffed into the windows, like faces that grin at me. Evenings, I break down and turn on the one in the TV room, but mostly I go naked and work on changing my attitude. Sweating is healthy, I tell myself, recognizing Momma in this strategy. She didn't believe in disappointment; she just convinced herself that she wanted whatever she got.

The cuckoo clock in the hall begins its hourly racket, and though I try, I can't stop myself from counting the cuckoos in my head—one, two, three, four, five, six, seven, eight—as I have done all my life. Just as the cuckoo jerks back inside and the little doors slam, a loud buzzing fills the house. I don't recognize the sound at first, and when I realize someone's at the door, I decide not to answer it. I'm naked, and by the time I put on clothes, whoever's there will be gone. I twirl the eggs with a spoon so that they spin in slow circles around the shiny bowl.

The doorbell keeps ringing, a punctual buzz-buzz, as though the person on the porch is sending Morse code. I begin to feel a little guilty, although I'm sure it's only some salesman or, worse yet, a Jehovah's Witness. After Mother died, I might as well have had "vulnerable" stamped on my forehead and a sign in the yard that said RELIGIOUS FANATICS STOP HERE. I collected a whole stack of *Watchtowers* on the coffee table, and once in a while I was even tempted to read them.

The buzzing stops, and a loud knocking begins. I give up, drop my spoon in the sea of yolks, and run to put on a T-shirt. The T-shirt's not really long enough to be decent, but I'm only planning on opening the door wide enough to say no.

When I peek out the little window in my front door, I see it's no salesman or Jehovah's Witness. She has no briefcase, no Bible, no pamphlets. Ready to leave, she hesitates on the edge of the porch. Her bare feet hang half-off, half-on, so that her balance is thrown back on her heels. She's wearing bright yellow shorts and a matching shirt – the kind of outfit you expect to see on a little girl – and she has arms and legs so long and lean that I clutch my own meaty thighs in dismay. Perched there, she stares out at the house across the street and the cars roaring by, as though the whole world is brand new to her.

And then the little boy who lives next door comes out and begins his daily routine. For an hour or more each morning, he rides his Big Wheel up and down the sidewalk. I bake my cheesecakes to the sound of plastic being ground away by concrete. He rounds the corner of his driveway and peddles past the woman on my porch, but she goes on staring across the street. I try to think what she's seeing – just an ordinary house, I know that – but what color is it? How many windows in the front? I keep failing these little quizzes. Yesterday I couldn't remember my mother's middle name. Eventually, it came back to me: Eileen. Helen Eileen Hobbs. Even so, I felt funny and disconnected. It's my mother's house I live in; her cheesecake recipe I bake every day; her wild cat who comes to the porch most evenings for scraps. My life is so closely connected to hers that I can't even think of my father except as her husband. Still, I can forget her middle name.

The woman on my porch leans forward, throwing herself off-balance so that she has to hop down the steps one after another. She smiles to herself, as though she's discovered a fun game, and I almost expect her to climb the stairs and start again. That's what I want her to do, but she keeps walking down the sidewalk. She's nearly to the street when I notice the coin purse and a section of the newspaper in the chair.

"Hey," I call out, opening the door, because I don't want her to leave. But she doesn't hear me. The little boy is on his way back now, his short legs pedaling faster and faster, the roar of his wheels drowning out my voice.

My T-shirt doesn't cover me, so all I can do is lean out a little farther and yell louder. But she doesn't turn around. She stops at the curb and looks up and down the street, for the bus maybe. Then she must remember her coin purse because she turns and catches me hanging out the door.

"Hello," I call out, feeling silly. Smiling, she walks toward me; her hands lift as though they're birds about to take flight; then, abruptly, she pulls them back to her sides.

"Did you knock?" I ask.

She nods and holds out the paper with the ad circled in purple marker. I reach out to take it, and the door swings open, exposing me. First, I crouch and yank at the shirt; then, slam the door and run for my pants. I expect she'll be gone by the time I return, but I find her squatting in the flower beds, examining the petals of the petunias and pansies. When she sees me, she stands and hands me the paper. It's my ad, but it's been running so long I've almost forgotten about it. Evidently, people don't rent rooms anymore. But putting the ad in the paper was only a gesture; I didn't expect anyone to answer it, and until now, no one has.

"Come in," I say, holding the door open. "You're welcome to see the room." The room I plan to rent is my old room. For the last year I've been living in Mother's room.

As I lead her down the long airless hall, I call out a warning.

"It'll be hot and dusty." She doesn't answer, but when I glance over my shoulder, she gives me another smile.

Even the cut-glass doorknob is warm. "It'll be hot," I try again. This time she nods. I push open the door and feel her fingers graze my back. It means nothing, I know, but I can't help being startled. No one has touched me in over a year.

We gasp as hot, dry air hits our faces. I spend several minutes trying to unstick the windows, and, while I grunt and heave, I imagine her leaving, those long legs carrying her down the hall, those bare feet coming down softly on the hardwood floors. Even after the windows are open, I go on standing with my back to her, giving her every chance.

But leaving is my idea, not hers. When I turn around, she's standing in the doorway, an anxious look on her face. Suddenly, I recognize it all: the alertness of her eyes, the way her head tilts slightly forward, her hands and fingers never quite still. She's afraid I've been talking, and she hasn't been able to read my lips. Does she just assume people will figure it out, I wonder. And then I remember the ones I've met in grocery store parking lots who have little cards and trinkets to sell. One way or the other. Either you pretend that you're like everyone else, or you announce that you're different. And she is one who pretends.

She moves about the room, running her fingers over the furniture, testing the mattress, but it's the two prints on the wall that hold her attention. They're by Degas, paintings of filmy ballerinas with pink flowers in their hair. Momma gave them to me on the morning of my seventh birthday, and they've been hanging in this same spot ever since.

She looks at them for some time, and when she turns away, there's a yearning, a restlessness about her. She points first to the pictures then to herself. Sounds come from her throat; I know they're words, but I can't make them out. She reminds me of a little girl trying to speak with the voice of her father. Not until I make sense of her gestures do I understand the words.

"Dancer, Libby's a dancer," she keeps saying.

"You're a dancer," I answer quietly, looking at Degas's ballerinas for the first time in years. Their bodies are indistinct, as though they're dancing in a dream.

* * *

I line up boxes in front of the closet. Then, before I can reconsider, I begin pulling things from hangers, one after another, and tossing them into the box behind me. Occasionally, I stop to examine a shirt or a sweater I can't remember wearing. Momma bought a lot of clothes. She bought them on credit, or she put them on layaway and paid for them piecemeal. She said she didn't notice it much that way. I'd come home from school and find these carefully arranged clothes on my bed. Momma would bend a sleeve on the shirt or ruffle the skirt so that it looked like some invisible girl was wearing them. I hated trying them on because it seemed to me that they looked better on the invisible girl than they ever would on me. When I modeled whatever it was—usually a skirt or a sweater—she always gave me the same smile, her big mouth turning up on each end so that she looked a little clownish. "Yes, very nice," she'd say, and after I retreated down the hall, she'd call out, "You'd better take care of that now."

They all look good as new. When the closet's empty, I tape the boxes closed and haul them out to the garage. Every time I go to the grocery store parking lot, I see that big box for the Salvation Army. That's where these clothes belong, but for the life of me, I can't bring myself to take them. Instead, I cover the boxes with a tarp because the roof leaks. Everything in the garage smells of mildew and rot. I suppose, eventually, the clothes will smell of it, too.

I'm expecting Libby; in fact, I've been waiting for her all morning. Still, she surprises me with her loud knock. When I open the door, she hurries in and I watch while she drops a big suitcase in the middle of the floor and gives it a kick. I know immediately what she's feeling. She reminds me of mimes I've seen on TV, only I think that maybe she's even more expressive.

"Did you take a taxi?" I ask.

She shakes her head, says "bus," and pretends to be riding one, jerking her head and shoulders before reaching out for the imaginary seat in front of her.

I smile because I don't know what to say. I'd like to compliment her, but I'm afraid she'll take offense.

Libby's wearing a leotard and cutoffs, and in the bedroom, where the light is better, I can see she's been sweating. Her hair's wet and combed straight back from her face, accentuating a widow's peak. I've never seen hair or eyebrows as black as hers; she looks stark. Nothing about her blends in – she's all motion and expression. Catching me studying her, she smiles and makes some signs I don't understand. Her hands are quick and fluid, and I think again of birds, how they can be sitting so still one instant then rise into the air the next.

I go over to the dresser and begin opening drawers to show her they're all empty. The drawers make hollow banging noises as I close them, and I feel strange, knowing I'm the only one who hears them. A small panic begins in me, and it grows as I open the closet. Although I want to look at Libby, I can't bring myself to turn around. I stare into the darkness of the closet and wonder how long before something happens. And then I decide to talk to her. It's a relief to think she can't hear me.

"I hope you won't think I'm crazy," I begin, my voice quiet, my eyes on the back wall of the closet. "It's just that my mother is the only person I've ever lived with. Since she died I've been here by myself. I hardly ever see anyone. Never had a real job." I reach up and rattle the empty hangers on the pole. "I guess I'm not your normal person, but I do want you here. Not just for the money either. I really want you here."

When I turn around Libby's sitting on the bed watching me. She has her shoes off and her feet tucked under her. Her back is straight, but she looks pale and very tired.

"You've been dancing?" I ask. I form the words slowly and exaggerate the movements of my lips and tongue.

She nods and motions for me to sit beside her. When I do, she puts her hand on my knee, looks into my eyes, and makes sounds I can't understand. Her attempts at speech take obvious effort, but the results are still flat, guttural, and often undecipherable. I stare at her blankly, and she tries again, then once again, those same sounds in that same loud, toneless voice. Finally, I shake my head.

Jumping up, she opens her suitcase and rifles through it until she finds a pencil and a pad.

I CAN TEACH YOU SIGNS FOR THE LETTERS OF THE ALPHABET, she writes, covering the page with big, unruly letters.

I grab the pencil and write WOULD YOU? Realizing what I've done, we both laugh.

"I forgot I can talk," I explain.

Libby smiles and nods, and then, almost as an afterthought, she touches my cheek with the tips of her fingers.

*   *   *

By ten o'clock at night the sky is so full of stars that even the darkness seems to shine. It's the best time of the day for watering; at least that's what my mother always said. She watered after dark to cut down on evaporation, but I water at night because it feels good. The yard is full of sounds — crickets, locusts, the occasional frog — but underneath the noise there's this stillness I feel I can rely on.

As I sit on the porch waiting to move the sprinkler, I think of going to bed with my windows open. While I sleep, the trees and grass will be soaking up moisture. It's a pleasant thought, and I stay with it for quite a while.

Somewhere down the alley a party is going on. Every now and then, laughter wafts down between the houses. And when I'm moving the sprinkler for the last time, a band begins warming up. Spurts of guitar, drums, and electric piano overwhelm my quiet backyard sounds. After positioning the sprinkler so it will spray the branches of the weeping willow, I walk across the damp grass to the back fence. In a minute, the band launches into an old song by the Rolling Stones. It's "I Can't Get No Satisfaction." The words are distorted, but the beat travels well, so I stand against the fence and listen. Truthfully, I'm not anxious to go inside. Even having Libby asleep in there does not kill the sensation I sometimes have that the house is more alive than I am, that it pulses with an awareness I mistake as my own.

Libby goes to bed early. She spends all her mornings and most of her afternoons dancing at the university. It's called The Summer Institute for Deaf Dancers, the first of its kind. Over and over she's told me how proud she is to be here, how this experience is a "great dream" come true. Yesterday afternoon, she showed me the sign for "dream." Her face was still flushed, and as she stretched out on the recliner, she arched her feet and tightened the muscles in her legs one last time before drifting off to sleep. I watched her sleep for several minutes and practiced the other signs she has shown me: "dance," "flower," "practice," "fast," "slow," "yes," "no." They're fun to do. Every day I learn a few more.

As I lean against the fence, I think about how hard she works and how utterly it absorbs her. But when summer's over, she'll go back to her typing job in New Jersey, back to being Libby Duncan, the girl who-would-have-been-a-beautiful-dancer. I wonder if this dead end bothers her as much as it bothers me.

The breeze picks up, and drops from the sprinkler spray across my back and down my legs. I turn to wipe them away and see Libby standing on the top step of the porch in her underwear. For a moment, all I see is the white of her bra and panties; then I can make out her arms moving slowly, like the shadows of tree limbs. I think her fingers are moving too. Is she talking to herself, I wonder. The music gets louder, and Libby hops down the steps, her body swaying in time to the beat. She must hear after all, I think, but then I remember what she has told me about music: she doesn't hear it, but she can feel it, like pulses, through the ground and in the air.

She doesn't see me, so I sidle over into the shadow of the garage and crouch close to the ground to watch. She's stamping her feet, raising her knees higher and higher, like some Indian lost in a war dance. Then, she reaches the center of the yard, and the tautness of her body goes suddenly slack. She seems about to fall before she breaks suddenly into a twirl. Her arms reach out and up; her body twists, twists; then, she hurls herself into the air. Once, she passes so close to me I can hear a soft rattle in her lungs as she pants. Even after the music dies away, and the crickets and frogs hold sway again, she go on weaving in and out of the trees. I hear an occasional splat-splat when the spray from the sprinkler hits her, and a little later I watch her leap and fall forward, slowly, as though she had control for that moment even over gravity.

In the morning, I find grass in the bottom of the tub, and as I bend to rinse it out I realize it's been days since I've thought of Momma.

The manager of The Garden Cafe asks if I can make a chocolate cheesecake. "I don't know," I answer.

"People come in and ask for it," he says. "Must be someone here in town making them."

"I'll try," I say. "When do you want it?"

"Soon," he tells me and turns away.

Pulling out of the parking lot, I wonder whether I can alter Momma's recipe. What would some melted chocolate do to the consistency? I feel a sudden unreasonable anger toward this man, and when I stop at a light, I realize I've gone half a mile in the wrong direction. I'm headed toward the university and away from my house. After the light turns green, I take the first right, but instead of going home, I turn again and come in behind the university. I'm going to watch Libby practice, but I don't admit this to myself until I begin circling the streets in search of a parking place.

It's been two years since I was last on campus. Momma was still alive then. I've taken a couple of classes over the years—Spanish, biology, English. Once I even enrolled in a ballet class, or maybe I only thought of enrolling. Either way, I'm sure I never went. The only class I ever finished was biology. It seems to me now that somebody else must have gone to those classes and told me about them, but I can't think who it would be.

Only lucky people park close to campus. I find a space six blocks away and go through the agony of parallel parking Momma's old '71 Continental. I've walked three blocks when I realize I don't know which building Libby is in. Not knowing which building is a good reason to go home. Any reason, no matter how flimsy, has been good enough in the past. I stop in the middle of the sidewalk, my heart pounding, that weightless feeling in my head. A ginger-colored cat watches me from the banister of the house across the street. The cat narrows his eyes and lengthens his body along the banister, stretching like an enormous furry caterpillar. The sun is directly overhead. I glance up at it, and when I look back at the cat, he's covered with green spots. The heat is a simple but convincing reason to keep walking.

Finding Libby is not as hard as I thought it would be. The dance building is new; I remember reading an article last year about the opening and dedication. I walk in what I think is the right direction and ignore all the older structures. The new buildings are clustered together, and by the time I ask a woman sitting in the grass, the building is in view. As she points it out, I thank her, and the world around me seems to brighten and sharpen by degrees.

The sound of drums takes me to her. I follow the noise up the stairs and down a long hallway to a door with a little window. When I look through, I see the practice room, all windows along one wall and all mirrors along the others. The polished floor reflects the bright colors the dancers wear: green, yellow, pink, red, blue. Degas should be alive to paint this, I think. The dancers are taking a break. About a dozen of them mill about, stretching their legs and waving their arms. One man jumps up and down, up and down. I expect him to stop, but he doesn't. Libby stands at the bar, one leg propped up, the other lean and straight as a flamingo's. She bends forward until her face touches the bar then raises up again. Her red leotard sticks to her back, and the bandana tied around her head is dark with sweat. After a few minutes, another woman comes over and touches her shoulder. They're beautiful together, Libby with her black hair and pale skin, and this other woman with her blonde hair tied up in a ponytail and a midsummer tan.

The woman begins signing, her hands a blur in the air. Libby smiles at first and nods repeatedly; emotions cross her face in quick succession: pleasure, anxiety, and finally tenderness. When the choreographer calls them back to practice, Libby gives her friend a quick hug, and as she does, her eyes stray to the door and seem to look directly into mine. Suddenly sick, I back away.

Momma always told me there's nothing worse than a spy, and she was talking about me. When I was a little girl, I used to hide in her closet. Sitting among her shoes in the dark was my way of being close to her. But she didn't want me to be close to her that way. Over and over, she dragged me out, both of us screaming. For a second, I expect Libby to burst through the door and drag me down the halls. But it doesn't happen. The dancers form a line, Libby on one end, and I find my way home.

*   *   *

By late afternoon it's so steamy outside that I retreat to the TV room, turn on the air conditioner, and watch reruns. Twice this week I've seen episodes I remember watching as a young girl. Now that the jokes are somewhat familiar, the shows are actually funnier. I feel a tenderness for Jethro and Lucy and Topper, faces from my past. I sit smiling at their antics until I doze off.

Usually, Libby takes a shower and eats something before coming in to talk with me, but today she knocks on the door first thing, waking me so that I look all dazed and silly when she opens the door. Her face is damp with sweat, but she smiles brightly, clearly glad to see me. Relieved, I wave her in.

She sighs, then plops down on the footstool in front of my chair and pulls the bandana from her head. I smell sweat and deodorant and something else I can't identify. Libby smoothes the bandana on her knee, folds it neatly, and turns her gaze to me. She's smiling, as though I've just given her the answer to a question. What is it? I wish Libby could hear, or else I wish for deafness, too. It occurs to me now that deafness might have helped with Momma. Maybe she wouldn't have expected so much. Maybe we would have gotten along. These thoughts surprise me. Not so long ago I told a pushy Pentecostal woman that Mother and I were uncommonly close. I remember holding up two fingers, one curled around the other, and seeing the pity on the woman's face, I burst into tears.

I am wondering what the truth might be when Libby begins finger spelling. She goes so fast I miss the first few words. My blank expression tells her to begin again, slower this time. When I concentrate, I catch most of what she tells me.

She's describing another dancer, a friend from the South who has wonderful golden hair. She spells out "shy," then cowers, a gesture so unlike her that it looks comical. She's bold and proud, expecting great things of the world and herself. I'd give my hearing in an instant to be like her.

"In trouble," she spells. Then she frowns, puzzled over how to go on.

Of course, it's the girl I saw her with today. I try to call her face

163

to mind but all I see is the flashing of her fingers against the green leotard and the pale shine of her hair.

Libby tells me the story of Anna and her boyfriend in Georgia, a "hearie" who rides a motorcycle and works at a discount store. They've been going together for a year, but he's never learned to sign. That's how Anna knows that she can't keep the baby.

"Has she told him she's pregnant?" I ask, and Libby shakes her head.

Evidently, Anna wasn't sure until a few weeks before the Institute. She hoped that all the dancing would take care of it. Now she worries that soon it may be too late.

"What do you mean, too late?" I ask.

Libby's face softens. "Before," she signs, then she presses her fingers against her belly and makes a delicate movement.

I nod and try to think what it would be like to feel something moving inside me. Babies are what I see other women pushing in strollers. So far as I can remember, I've never even held one.

"She wants an abortion?" The clinic on Duvall is about a mile from a restaurant that buys my cheesecakes. I pass it every day. Sometimes people are picketing, carrying signs that say things like GOD DOESN'T BELIEVE IN ABORTION. Once, I passed a young girl sitting on the curb crying. Her purse lay open beside her; the contents were rolling into the street.

Libby makes the nod with her fist that means "yes" then spells out "help."

It's the question she wants me to answer.

I stare at the television screen. A commercial is on, and I pretend interest to give myself more time. I feel sick to my stomach now, and my throat's beginning to close as I answer.

"I'll try, Libby."

* * *

Anna lives in a small apartment complex within walking distance of the university. The outside doors are only a couple of steps apart, and I can imagine the tiny dark studios built for students who only come home to sleep. Restless, frenetic people, I tell myself. I wouldn't want to be like them. One comes home as I wait — a lean young man, shirtless and carrying a tennis racket. I watch as he disappears behind his orange door.

The parking lot is shady, and I don't mind waiting. Libby explained that all she really needs is transportation. Anna will be weak afterwards. It didn't seem like much to ask. Cars swish past; heat flies off the wheels and into my open window. I turn my face away and am not surprised when the young man emerges, wearing a shirt and carrying a notebook. It's ten in the morning, and we've just delivered my cheesecakes. As I sit listening to the car radio, a dense pleasure catches me off-guard. All Libby's doing. This morning she helped me mix the cream cheese and eggs. Later, she admired the neatly staggered pans through the window in the oven door. I'm thinking about how I'll miss her when she emerges with Anna from one of the second story doors. They stand on the landing, smiling and waving at me. I start the motor.

* * *

We don't go to the clinic I pass every day. This one is hidden away in the same building with an optometrist and a dentist. Outside, a lone protester stands like a sentry; inside, the walls are painted cool pastels and the hallway is strewn with rag rugs. Someone has struggled to give this place a homey feel.

Anna has a 10:45 appointment, but around 11:00 I realize that her appointment does nothing more than assure her a place in line. The room overflows with women, but since we arrived, only one name has been called. A woman beside me keeps sighing and checking her watch.

Anna holds a magazine in her lap. She tries to read, but now and then I catch her studying the women around her. One is visibly pregnant, and Anna's eyes fix on her. Even after the woman notices and shifts in her seat, Anna keeps staring.

"What are you looking at?" the woman finally asks. Her voice isn't loud, but the room is so quiet that everyone looks up.

I wonder if Anna has read her lips and how she will respond. I expect her to look away, but she doesn't. She goes on staring, her gaze stiff, almost befuddled.

"She's deaf," I say, and everyone in the room turns to me.

"What?" the woman asks. She's older than the others, and I'd bet this isn't her first unwanted pregnancy. Waiting for her at home are more children she didn't really want.

"She doesn't hear what you're saying," I explain, pointing to my own ear. "It's nothing personal. She's scared, that's all."

Several of the other women nod, keeping their eyes on me and away from Anna. Libby signs "thank you" — the same sign that means "good" — and takes Anna's hand.

In a few minutes the nurse calls the woman's name. She rises slowly, but instead of following the nurse, she comes over to Anna. The blouse she's wearing is snug around the belly, and she tugs at it before she speaks.

"I'm sorry," she says. Her hand reaches out, as though she wants to touch Anna's hair. "It's just that I knew what you were thinking."

Anna nods and makes several signs I don't understand. The woman seems satisfied because she turns and walks away with the nurse. When the door closes behind them, Anna picks up her purse and motions for us to follow.

Out in the hall, she leans against the pale blue wall. She's panting, and her eyes are squeezed shut. She signs, "too late, too late."

Libby shakes her until she opens her eyes, then asks if she felt the baby move. Anna shakes her head. She looks at both of us, then down at the floor.

"I feel *her* baby," she finally signs. Libby and I stand stupidly, not sure how to respond.

"Okay," Libby signs at last. "Let's go."

* * *

An old movie is on. Libby and Anna sit on the couch and stare politely at the screen. I wonder if they'd watch it if I weren't for me? At least it's cool, but the window unit rumbles so loudly it sometimes drowns out the actors' voices: then, I, too, am watching a movie without sound. Surely they're bored. I get up and go into the kitchen to cut thick slices of cheesecake. This one is experimental. I mixed melted Hershey bars in the batter, and I'm looking for reactions. It cuts easily and holds its shape on the plate. So far, so good.

When I return with the tray, Libby and Anna stand in front of the television, and the room is alive with music. Notes swell and beat around my ears. My heart pounds. The melody's familiar — Tchaikovsky I think. Libby has her hand on the volume knob, and she's turned it up as loud as it will go. Anna touches her arm and they move apart. Then, I can see the screen. It's classical ballet; a whole corps of dancers cover the stage. Their movements suggest the music: I can predict every leap and twirl, but not the grace or energy, not the beauty. As the music slows, the priniipal dancers slide into an effortless arabesque, and while I watch, Libby and Anna slide with them. Both lean forward at precisely the same instant and hold the stance until the dancers on the screen move out of it.

Afterwards, I turn the volume down and go get them some water. In the minute or two it takes me, they eat halfway through the cheesecake.

"How do you like it?" I'm looking for honest feedback.

They go on eating then hold out their plates for more.

"Could you hear the music?" I ask when they're finished.

They shake their heads. I'm surprised. I assumed they must have heard at least a whisper of it.

"What was it like?" Anna asks.

I shrug. How can you describe a particular piece of music to someone who's never heard music at all?

"Different as it went along," I say. When I can, I use signs, sometimes making them up to get my point across, but mostly they have to read my lips. "At first, the music was smooth and deep, like a lake you can't see the bottom of. Then it got stronger and more turbulent, the way a storm blows in and makes waves on the lake. Have you ever stood at the window and watched a wild storm?" They both nod, and Libby reaches for Anna's hand. "You know how you start to feel wild yourself, like the storm's becoming part of you? And then later when it passes, the birds start to sing, and you know exactly how the birds feel, too? That's kind of like the music."

I wait for their response, but they go on holding hands and looking at me, as though they think I'm not finished.

"I guess I can't explain it," I say.

Libby leans over and squeezes my knee, hard. "Thank you," she signs, and then "beautiful."

*   *   *

I wake when the clock in the hallway strikes three. My eyes open as the last chime dies away, and I lie listening to the silence then get up and walk the length of the house to the bathroom.

Libby usually sleeps with her door closed, but tonight, perhaps because Anna's visiting, she's left the door ajar. I stop outside the room and look in at them. It's a hot night, so they aren't using the sheet. Anna wears a T-shirt, Libby nothing at all. Moonlight shines in the window, highlighting the nape of a neck, stretches of leg. How lovely they look, tangled together like a pair of exhausted lovers. My breath catches in my throat, and I remember Libby's hand searching for Anna's, the grace and urgency of her fingers. Then I think of this afternoon when Anna stood outside the clinic and told us she'd felt another woman's baby. Drawn to their bedside, I peer down at Anna's flat stomach. I look for some sign, but the baby is still a secret. Anna shifts and tucks her chin close under Libby's arm. I step back, though what I want is to lie down beside them.

The light from the window shines on Degas's dancers. I can make out one frothy skirt then a pale arm and hand reaching upward. Even as Momma hammered the nails and hung the heavy frames on my wall, I knew somehow we'd both be disappointed. But tonight she has her wish: beautiful dancers are sleeping in my bed.

*   *   *

The crowd is larger than I expected. The seats are full. I twist in my seat, surrounded by a sea of faces. An usher hurries past, searching for singles. Who are all these people, I wonder, and how did they end up at a recital for deaf dancers? My hands lie quietly in my lap, and I wear one of Momma's best dresses. As I strain to hear the comments of those around me, I begin to feel important. I know two of the performers. One is my best friend.

Finally, the lights dim, and then go out. We sit in the darkness, suddenly hushed, and listen as the heavy swish of drapery brushes against wood. After the curtain opens, the thud of the dancers' feet punctuates the silence. Like the rest of the audience, I lean forward and peer through the darkness to see them. In a minute, the lights come up, and the dancers start to move. Still no music. Just when I've decided this will be a silent performance, the drums boom, and we jump in our seats.

Libby stretches and curls, but the stiff way she holds her head tells me she's scared. Anna's dancing is more practiced, less instinctual than Libby's. While I watch Anna moving in and out of a row of motionless dancers, I imagine a life for her—a golden-haired little girl and a new man, someone who'll be captivated by them. It's not hard to imagine.

Libby's the last in a line of frozen dancers, and when the others have all begun to move again, she still stands alone at the end of the stage. I wait for her to move, and when she doesn't, I tap my heels on the concrete floor. Move, Libby, I command her, sure that nerves are keeping her rooted. But she's only waiting for her moment, and when it comes she's off running, circling the stage in long leaps, a bird learning to fly.

* * *

Tonight it's so cool I don't need the air conditioner in the TV room. A wonderful breeze brushes against my skin. I sit naked in the armchair and watch two movies and part of another one. I've been watching lots of TV since Libby left; that's one way I know I miss her. The other way I know is that yesterday I packed up the two prints by Degas—frames and all—and shipped them to her. It cost an arm and a leg, and still they couldn't assure me that the glass wouldn't get broken. But like the guy said, they have glass in New Jersey.

It's nearly eleven by the time I go out to move the sprinkler. The crickets and cicadas are quieter tonight. They must be waning, like the moon. It's just a chip of light in the sky, and I have to wait on the porch until my eyes adjust to what at first seems like painted darkness. In a while, I can trace the branches of the willow undulating in the cool night air; later, I recognize the dull gleam of the metal fence and catch occasional flashes of light on the garage windows. It's enough to set me at ease, and as I step off the porch and onto the wet grass, I feel a sense of belonging I've never felt before. It begins as a vague contentment, an enjoyment of the wet, tickling sensation on the soles of my feet, but as I move the sprinkler and stand listening to the spray beating lightly on the leaves of the willow, it grows inside me until I must rise up on the balls of my feet and stretch my arms skyward.

Sharon Oard Warner was born and raised in Dallas, Texas. She received a B.A. in philosophy from The University of Texas at Austin and M.A. in English/Creative Writing from the University of Kansas. Her stories have been published in a number of literary magazines including *The Sonora Review, The Gamut, The Long Story, Green Mountains Review*, and *Iowa Woman*. She teaches at Drake University and lives in Ames, Iowa with her husband, Teddy, a psychologist, and their sons Corey and Devin.

About her writing, Warner says: "Writing is an adventure for me. When I begin, it's because there's something I don't understand—a person, an issue, an emotion, or an image. My stories are like jigsaw puzzles in unmarked boxes. I start with one piece and trust that when I put it down, another will follow. Eventually, if I'm patient, the whole picture emerges. The process is immensely satisfying, and since there are so many things I don't understand, I never worry about running out of material."